I0527329

Duncan MacNab

Archaeological Dissertation

on the birth-place of Saint Patrick

Duncan MacNab

Archaeological Dissertation
on the birth-place of Saint Patrick

ISBN/EAN: 9783337335809

Printed in Europe, USA, Canada, Australia, Japan

Cover: Foto ©Andreas Hilbeck / pixelio.de

More available books at **www.hansebooks.com**

DUBLIN

Printed by James Moore,
2 CRAMPTON-QUAY.

THE BIRTH-PLACE OF SAINT PATRICK.

THE elegant essay on the "Birth Place of St. Patrick, by J. Cashel Hoey," edited, along with other essays in 1865, by H. E. Manning, D.D., contains interesting information relative to the extant manuscripts of St. Patrick's Confession; and to other documents bearing on the subject in discussion. It also gives some account of old Roman roads and ruins in the neighbourhood of Desvres. The air of candour and straight-forwardness with which the author undertakes his task, at once engages the attention and the favour of his reader. Under the guidance of authority, Mr. Hoey sought, in the vicinity of Dumbarton, on the Clyde, in Scotland, to identify some of the places mentioned in the Confession; and, having failed in the attempt, he adopted Dr. Lanigan's opinion that St. Patrick was born in France, in the Pas de Calais, at Boulogne-sur-Mer.

Unfortunately for the truth of history, Dr. Lanigan considered the birth of St. Patrick in a particular locality not simply as an historical *fact*, to be ascertained and proved by ancient records; but as a theory, to be unfolded and sustained by geographical and etymological arguments. Accordingly, he accommodated facts and dates to his theory. When, in the biographies of St. Patrick, he met with incidents at variance with his theory, he ascribed them to the invention, the credulity, or the ignorance of the writers, whilst he admitted favorable statements on the assertion of one biographer, even when contradicted by others of equal, or of greater weight. At times he altered, *ad libitum*, the expressions of his authorities into what he tells us they intended, or ought to have written; and then he tries to establish facts by these gratuitous assumptions. (1)

Although Mr. Hoey has avoided many of Lanigan's errors, still he views his subject in the same light; (2) and, therefore, (notwithstanding the refutation of Lanigan's assertions by Daniel Rock, D.D., published as the first appendix to his letter to Lord John Manners) he undertakes "to perfect the proof which Dr. Lanigan had commenced;" and, he endeavours to do so, mainly by the aid of etymology and geography. Like a man of business, with one sweeping sentence he clears the ground of Don Philip O'Sullivan, of the Breviary of Rouen, and of all such as would maintain that St. Patrick was a Breton of Brittany—" this theory, however, falls summarily to the ground, when it is opposed to the fact that the province now known by the name of Brittany, was not inhabited by any tribe which bore the name in the time of St. Patrick;"—then, as if master of the field, he cites Dr. Lanigan, who confidently asserts that " Bonavem, or Bonaven, was in Armoric Gaul, being the same town as Boulogne-sur-Mer in Picardy."

Sixty-three or sixty-six biographies of St. Patrick have been written, yet his early history seems extremely confused and uncertain. (3) Some have denied his existence, while others have gifted him with a specious ubiquity. He is said to have been born in Scotland, in Wales, in Ireland, in Flanders, and in Brittany! If there be another point of history obscured by a cloud of writers, it is that which refers to the names of the sea-port towns in the Pas de Calais.

Dr. Lanigan informs us, on the authority of Valesius, that the name of Boulogne itself was changed from *Gessoriacum* to *Bononia*, about the time of Constantine the Great;

that the *Iccius Portus* was by Culverius thought to be the same as Gessoriacum, or Boulogne; that Horsley would have it to be the Port of Calais; and that Boudrand and Camden would make it *Witsant* or *Vissent* or *Esseu*. Pinkerton says it was also called *Bonona*. (4) Dr. Lanigan quotes Baxter to show that Bononia is etymologically the same as Bonium. (5) According to Mr. Hoey, *it is very possible* that Bonaven may have been originally written *Bononen*. He also informs us, that " eighty-eight different works have been written to settle the site of the Portus Itius, whence Cæsar embarked to invade Britain, and nineteen different localities assigned." Dr. Lanigan and Mr. Hoey had engaged out of this darkness to bring light, and they have only managed to convert it into chaos. For the success of their efforts they relied mainly on one word of St. Feich's hymn (Emtur) and, on one sentence from the Confession of St. Patrick. (6)

How have they succeeded?

They looked for purely Celtic names, one of them having a Latin inflection, in a district where Roman or Romanised names had been in use for four centuries previous to the period of their enquiries. The result is exactly what might have been foreseen. Historians and geographers say "French or Gaulish Armorica"—these gentlemen say "Armoric Gaul," as if Armorica contained Gaul. St. Patrick says *Bonaven Taberniæ*—Mr. Hoey replies, Bononienses Taberniæ, meaning Tabernæ Bononienses, or Bononiæ. St. Feich says Emtur—Hoey, Tournehem—St. Patrick, Bonaven—they, Gessoriacum—Bononia. St. Patrick **writes** Taberniæ—Lanigan declares that means Tervanna. No, exclaims Mr. Hoey, it is too remote from Boulogne—thirty miles—it is now called St. Pol. Well, Lanigan names Taruanna. No, again, repeats Mr. Hoey, that is Therouenne—twenty miles still farther off— it must be Desvres, which was called Divernia in the low Latin of the middle ages, long **after** St. Patrick's time. St.

Patrick has Enon—Hoey says Enna—Lanigan is silent. Four of the lives in Colgan's collection mention a town Nempthur—Lanigan will not admit its existence as a town; but he receives it from Probus as a province. Mr. Hoey considers Lanigan has erred in rejecting Nempthur as a town, and, therefore, while he retains it as a province, he has it also as a town. St. Feich applies Emtur to Bonaven (St. Patrick's birth-place), and Mr. Hoey connects it with Enon, whence the saint was led into captivity. As the historian and the essayist agree neither with their authorities nor with one another, nor yet are always consistent with themselves, they surely presume too much, I do not say on the gullibility of the public, but on the ignorance and credulity of the more intelligent class of their readers, when they expect them to receive this theory, thus developed and completed, as decisive.

In order to maintain their position, they tell us, that St. Patrick preached at Boulogne against Pelagianism—that Boulogne is etymologically, and in fact, a town on the mouth of a river; and, therefore, the Bonaven of St. Patrick's Confession; —that it was connected, according to Lanigan, with Tervanna, Taruanna, or Tarabanna, because those places at some time were parts of the Episcopal see of Boulogne; or, according to Mr. Hoey, with Desvres, by a Roman road; that Enon means a *river house*, or *river lodge*, and is the same as the village Enna. Mr. Hoey also assures us, that Emtur, or Nemtur, is no other place than Tournehem, *i. e.*, the tower of Em; that those places were in the province of Neustria; that St. Patrick was one of a Gaulish tribe called Britanni, and was led captive into Ireland by Niall Naoigiallach. Boulogne, they say, was called Gessoriacum, Bonaven, Bonaun; also Bonon, and Bononia, and, perhaps, Bononon. But their reference to authority shows only Gessoriacum and Bononia. (7)   To prove that Boulogne is the same as Bonaven, they quote Bullet, who says that *Am*, *Avon*, *On*, in Celtic, signify a river, and *Bon*, a mouth; and that the town was so called from its being at the mouth of a river.

In the dialect of the Celtic with which I am best acquainted, *Bun* means a root. (8) From *Bun* we have *Bonn*, a base or foundation; and the term *Bun*, sometimes in composition *Bon*, is applied to the mouth of a river metaphorically, as to its base or broadest part. Avon is written *Amhain*, and is the nearest Celtic form to the Latin cognate word *Amnis*. To those who know anything of Celtic it is evident, even without the authority of Bullet, that Amhain, Afon, Avon, Aven, Aun, Aw, and On, are what philologists term phonetic corruptions, or different dialectic forms of the same word, signifying a river.

It is not, however, equally clear that Bonaven and Boulogne are the same. First, because it is uncertain to what extent we are to look for Celtic words or roots in the names of places in Belgic Gaul. As Hecatæus, 500 B.C., and, after him, Heredotus, Democritus, and even Strabo, include Belgic Gaul in the Celtica, or country of the Celts, (9) the names of some places in that district are, likely, of Celtic origin, but not all. For we learn from Cæsar that the languages of the Celtic and Belgic Gauls were different, and that the Belgic were of German extraction. (10) The subsequent settlement of the Francs in Belgic Gaul must also have considerably altered the names of its various localities. Secondly, because Boulogne is but the French of Bononia; and the argument drawn from the word Bononia is inadmissible: since Boulogne was not so called till the Celtic had been nearly forgotten in that country, and superseded, first, by the Teutonic, and, afterwards, by the Latin. The first is clear from Cæsar's testimony; the second is proved by the philological affinity existing between the Latin and the French. If, then, we take into consideration the practice common to immigrants of giving to their new settlements the names of the places which they have left, the German origin of the Belgæ, and Webster's etymology of Bononia, we will be forced to recognise in it the Bonona of the Iceni, and to remit the name and its interpretation to Bonn, upon the Rhine. Thirdly, because the most ancient name of Boulogne—Gessoriacum, may readily be derived from the Celtic Gear (pronounced Ger), short, and Srothan (Sroan), a streamlet; but never from Avon. Add to this the fact that the Laine, which enters the sea at Boulogne, is not a river, but a brook, which a man can leap across where its channel is not artificially formed. (11) Fourthly, because etymological derivation, as used by *Bullet, Lanigan, and Hoey*, is so capricious that nothing can be decided by it, and least of all a disputed point of history. The following specimens of Bullet's derivations are given by Pinkerton in his Dissertation on the Goths, from what he designates an "insane work," the *Memoirs de la langue Celtique*, par M. Bullet, Besançon, 1754, 3 vols. folio; "such are Northampton (North Hampton), from Nor, the mouth of a river; Tan, a river; Ton, habitation: Northill (North Hill), from Nor, a river, and Tyne, habitation: Ringwood, from Ren, a division; in, a river; and hed, a forest: Uxbridge (Ouse Bridge), from uc, a river; and brig, a division. *Risum teneatis!* "

Mr. Hoey, after laughing at Colgan, for referring Taberniæ to a Roman Camp, considers it, himself, as a military station, as appears from his commentaries and his explanation of Taberniæ; while Lanigan sees in it Tarabanna. Finally, because, even supposing that Boulogne has the same meaning as Bonaven, the case is not decided. For there are, elsewhere, towns and villages at the mouths of rivers, and some of them called by the same name. For example: Bologne, or Bononia, in Aquitain; Bologna, in Italy; and at least two on the west coast of Scotland, Bunawe, on Loch Etive, about ten miles from Oban; and Bannavie, on the Lochy, near the west end of the Caledonian Canal.

Probus, whose life of St. Patrick Dr. Lanigan prefers to all the others, says that the Saint's native village was situated " haud procul a mari," *i.e.*, at a short distance from the sea. This expression is conclusive against Boulogne-sur-Mer.

From the text of St. Patrick's Confession it evidently appears that Bonaven by itself cannot indicate the place of his birth. Bonaven must be taken in connection with Tabernia—Bonaven Taberniæ. This has given occasion to Mr. Hoey to explain Tabernia by Desvres—Bononienses Taberniæ (Tabernæ)—and to tell us that they were connected by a road; and to Dr. Lanigan to mention Tervanna, Taruanna, or Tarrabanna, as parts of the Episcopal See of Boulogne. Neither their explanations of the diversity, or rather their metamorphosis, of names, nor yet the connection they indicate as subsisting between those different places, is satisfactory. We cannot look on London as a dependency of John O'Groat's House, although there is a road from the one to the other; nor can we admit of Sutherlandshire as being a part of Iceland or of Lapland, although it constitutes a portion of the Prefecture Apostolic of the Arctic Regions.

Dr. Lanigan and Mr. Hoey are agreed that Bonaven, Enon, Nemtur, Armorica, and Letha, are Celtic words, and they have condescended to explain them; they have also used their interpretation to determine the geographical and tropological position of those places. Yet neither of them has recognised Tabernia as Celtic, although it has in Latin quite as barbarous or Celtic an aspect as any or all of the other words. Tabernia is as clearly Celtic as Hibernia—*I-Erin*— *i.e.*, the island of Erin. Tabh-Erin, or Tab'-Erin, *i.e.*, the sea of Erin. Tabernia may also, though not so naturally, be resolved into *Taob'-Erin;* for, in *Taob',* a side, *ao* is a diphthong whose sound according to the different provincial dialects or accents is approximated by the Latin *a* or *u*, but cannot be expressed by *ao* pronounced separately and distinctly. Bonaven Taberniæ, then, means literally the mouth of a river of the Irish Sea; or the mouth of a river contiguous to Ireland. That part of the Atlantic, which at the present day is known as the Irish Sea, was so called long before the time of St. Patrick; as we learn from the geographer Ptolomy, of Alexandria, who flourished in the second century of the Christian æra. Thus we see that, even under etymological guidance, Bonaven Taberniæ must be sought at the mouth of some British river flowing into the Irish Sea. Enon must also be in Britain as it was near Bonaven.

We cannot suppose St. Patrick, a nobleman of Roman descent, to have been ignorant of the Roman name of the town in which he was born. If he wrote his Confession in Latin—and we have no evidence to the contrary—if the place had such a name he would have used it; unless it were better known by its purely Celtic appellation. Such might easily have been the case in certain parts of Britain which had never been, or but for a very short time, under the power of the Romans. But not in France, especially about Boulogne, for that territory had been part of a Roman province for 400 years, and the Roman or Latinised names of its towns were better known, when St. Patrick wrote, than they are now. Had he meant those places he would have written Gessoriacum, or Bononia, Tervanna, or Taruanna, or Tabernæ Bononienses, and Enna. The exact repetition of Bonaven Taberniæ in all the copies of his Confession shows that the words have come down to us as they were written by St. Patrick.

What are we to think of St. Feich's Emtur, which Dr. Lanigan has changed into Neustria, and Mr. Hoey into Tournehem?

Lanigan says it ought to be written Nemhthur, as it is by Colgan, and by those who interpret it Holy or Heavenly Tower. He also adds—" Nemhthur, according to Irish pronunciation, must be read Nevthur, whereas the letter *m*, with *h* added to it, or a point placed over it, is pronounced like *v*;" supposing Nemthur or Nemhthur to be derived from the word for *heaven*—in Irish and Scotch Gaelic, *Neamh*, gen. *Neimh*; in Welsh, *Név*.—Dr. Lanigan so far offers no great violence to the language, as the proper form of the word would be Neamhthùr. (12) But so much cannot be said when, from Nemhthur, he converts it into Nepthur and Nephthur. For when, in the inflection of a Celtic word, a consonant is aspirated by the addition of an *h*, it should not be altered into another letter, but retained to indicate the root and preserve the meaning. He does, indeed, reject the signification *heavenly*, yet without perceiving the force of the ridiculous alteration he has made; for there is no Celtic word beginning with Nep; and the only word approaching to it (wherever it comes from) to be found in the Gaelic dictionaries is Néip or Neup, *i.e.* a turnip; Nepthur or Nephthur in Celtic can only mean a turnip-tower. St. Feich wrote in Irish, and all who have written of Nemthur have treated it as a Celtic word. Even Dr. Lanigan begins his alterations of it by Celtic pronunciation, orthography, and etymology. Having made it Nephthur, Nepthur, he next changes it into Neptricum, then into Neptria, and lastly into Neustria, and explains it by the English words New Land. Of course these last changes having been made *in nubibus*, he may think them not far removed from Neamlithùr, or Heavenly Tower.

He lays great stress on Probus calling Nevtria a province —*provincia*, but very foolishly; for Probus wrote in the Latin of the middle ages, when the term *provincia* was applied to any tract of country; and there is no surer way of erring than to apply classical interpretation to mideval Latin. (13) The passage referred to in the work of Probus shows clearly that the author never meant the French province of Neustria. (14) " Saint Patrick, who was also called Socket, was by nation a Briton. He was born in Britain—in the village of Bannave, of the district Taburnia, not far from the western sea, which village we have unquestionably found to be of the province of Nevtria or Nentria, where of old the giants are said to have dwelt." The term *Brito* is applicable only to the natives of Britain, or their descendants, the inhabitants of Bretagne. So also Britanniæ, in the plural, signifies only Great Britain. Whoever heard of giants living in the neighbourhood of Boulogne?

I have next to consider Mr. Hoey's explanation of Nemthur. On the authority of Professor Eugene O'Curry, who minutely examined the oldest extant manuscript of St. Feich's hymn, preserved in the British museum, he tells us that, though generally written Nemtur, it ought to be Emtur, as it is in some of the Breviaries. I believe this statement to be correct. What is Mr. Hoey's interpretation of Emtur? "The word, then, means not Holy Tower, but the tower of some place or person indicated by the word Em." According to him, Tournehem, *i. e.*, the Tower of the river Em, or Hem. I cannot accept either this interpretation or its application. Not the latter, because, in effecting the transformation of Emtur into Tournehem, of his own accord, without reason or authority, he has added the river Em or Hem. Not the former, because *em* is only the Celtic definite article; so that Emtur means simply *the tower;* Nemtur, or Nentur, *of the towers.* (15)

The whole difficulty regarding Emtur has arisen from the use of agglutination, and ignorance or imperfect knowledge of the Celtic language. By agglutination, pronouns are joined to verbs, sometimes also the auxiliary verb to that which it helps to form; prepositions are united to nouns, and also coalesce with pronouns; and occasionally the last letter of a word is prefixed to the succeeding word. (16) In the Irish translation of the Imitation of Christ, chap. i. p. 1, I find "*Andorchadas*" for *an dorchadas.* In the Book of Ballymote I see "*iseatso*" for *is eat so*, and many other instances of agglutination. I need not, however, wander from my subject for an illustration, as Dr. Rock supplies me from

O'Connor with the Irish text of St. Feich's hymn—" Genair Patraic i Nemthur," which Dr. O'Connor translates, " Natus est Patricius Nemturri." Freed from agglutination, the Irish text would stand thus: " Genair Patraic in em thur;" or, as corrected by Professor O'Curry, " Genair Patraic in em tùr." This means literally—" Genitus est Patricius in turri:" Patrick was begotten in the tower. I must admit, however, that *am* or *em* is not always now the definite article. When it comes between the preposition *in*, or *ann*, and a noun, it is frequently only what grammarians call an euphonic particle, but which appears to be used like an indefinite article. (17) As, however, I have no means of knowing the ideas of euphony entertained by St. Feich and other Irish Celts in his time, I have no reason for setting down the *em* here in question as anything else than the definite article. I have, on the contrary, a special reason, which will be seen hereafter, for believing that it was used as such by the saintly poet. If *em* were here simply an euphonic particle, the sense of the text would be—Patrick was begotten in a tower. Although this is all that the poetry of St. Feich supplies; yet, it is quite possible that St. Patrick's Bonaven might have had another name like Nempthur or Emptor mentioned in the Breviaries and Biographies. That, however, is another question for future consideration.

Having now discussed the etymological evidence adduced by Mr. Hoey and Dr. Lanigan, I may be permitted to remark that they have not succeeded by this means in identifying any one of the places mentioned in St. Patrick's Confession, or St. Fiech's Hymn; but have only found places bearing somewhat similar names. That, however, is no proof—at any rate, without the sanction of historical authority—or if it be, they might as well maintain that St. Patrick was a Jew. They could say that he was a Christian, that the Christians came originally from Judea; and show, with fewer changes of letters and of words, that Bonaven was Bethsaida on the

Jordan; Tabernia, Tiberias; Enon, Ænon; and Nemtur, Mount Tabor.

I will now examine their geographical arguments. Dr. Lanigan, having converted St. Feich's Emtur and Probus's Nevtria or Nentria into the French province Neustria, asserts, and so does Mr. Hoey, that it stretched from the Loire to the Meuse. But they are certainly mistaken; for this extension of Neustria leaves no room for the province of Austrasia, which occupied the space between the Meuse and the Somme. (18)

Erroneously assuming or believing that St. Patrick was first led into captivity from Armorica, and knowing that he had been captured at Enon; and, having placed Enon in the territory of Boulogne; they next give undue extension to Armorica. They cite Lobineau to prove that the whole coast from the Pyrenees to the Rhine was anciently called Armorica. Unquestionably it might have been so when that tract of country was inhabited by the Celts; but, as we have learned from Cæsar, that was altered long before St. Patrick's time, when the Germans took possession of Belgic Gaul; (19) and Gaul, properly so called, was the country between the Garonne and the Seine. (20) The coast of Belgic Gaul was distinct from Armorica, (21) and known by a different name —*Tractus Nervicanus.* (22) Yet to support their theory, and bring Boulogne and Enna within the Tractus Armoricanus, Dr. Lanigan and Mr. Hoey now ignore the existence of the *Tractus Nervicanus*, as they before annihilated Austrasia to make room for their overgrown Neustria.

There was, as they say in Gaul, a tribe called Britanni. Pliny mentions them, and Sanson and Carte have written diffusely concerning them. Boulogne and its neighbourhood was possessed by a tribe called Morini. The territory of the Britanni was situated not on the Liane, but on the Somme. Of this Mr. Hoey was well aware, for, in a note, he quotes a passage from `Hardion defining their position. (23) We do not read, however, of their having given their name to the country they occupied. It was not called Britannia, much less Britanniæ. If St. Patrick had been one of that tribe his Bonaven should have been not Boulogne, on the Liane, but Abbeville, on the Somme; and he would have been called Britannus instead of Brito. So precise and definite is the meaning of the word *Brito* that even Dr. Lanigan considers the dispute relative to the native country of the heresiarch Pelagius definitively settled by its application to him by St. Prosper, and therefore concludes that Pelagius was a Scotchman. (24)—" Pelagius Brito.' *Vide* Lanigan, vol. i., p. 16.

That Dr. Lanigan, and Mr. Hoey have found it necessary to support their etymological and geographical arguments by a reference to the historical fiction of St. Patrick having been led into captivity from Armorica by a thrice murdered king, Niall Naoighiallach, is of itself a strong indication of the insufficiency of their proof, and a fit conclusion of their thesis. Niall is said to have been first killed by a poisoned arrow shot across the Loire, A.D. 398, (25) subsequently by one shot across the Liane, in 404, (26) and lastly, according to Mr. Hoey, " on the sea of Iccius, between France and England." (27) Although it is of no consequence by what Irish chief St. Patrick was captured, and he might as well have been seized by the said Niall as by any other Irish pirate, Dr. Lanigan has deducted four years from the shortest period of life assigned by any of his authorities to St. Patrick; and thus he is enabled to place his birth in 387, so that the time of his captivity may correspond with Niall's last expedition and his death, which as I have mentioned, is said by some to have occurred in France.

The crowning achievement of this piratical excursion is yet to be observed. St. Patrick says in his Confession that he was made captive along with several thousand others. (28) But this dead Irish chieftain effected his purpose with such secrecy that the forcible abduction into Ireland of so many thousands of Belgic Gauls was quite unknown to their countrymen, and consequently has never been mentioned by any French chronicler or historian. Their landing in Ireland must have been equally mysterious, for though the Irish Annals mention Niall's death, " *occ muir in ioct*," they say nothing of his thousands of Gaulish captives. The only parallel to this exploit that I have read in history, is the ferrying, by the living, of the souls of the dead, from the opposite shores to Britia, described by Procopius.—De Bello Gothico, l. iv., cap. 20.

Mr. Hoey relates that, of the 420 churches in the ancient diocese of Boulogne, eighty-two were dedicated to St. Martin, several to St. Maclan, and to St. Killan, but none to St. Victricius, whom he suspects to be St. Patrick. Had St. Patrick been born at Boulogne this statement would appear as singular as the following extract from Chambers's Book of Days:—

" Here we are reminded of a very remarkable fact in connection with geographical appellations, that the footsteps of St. Patrick can be traced almost from his cradle to his grave, by the names of the places called after him. Thus, assuming his Scotch origin, he was born at Kilpatrick, (cell or church of Patrick,) in Dumbartonshire. He resided for some time at Dalpatrick, (the district or division of Patrick), in Lanarkshire, and visited Crag Phadrig, (the rock of Patrick), near Inverness. He founded two churches—Kirkpatrick, at Irongray, in Kirkcudbright—and Kirkpatrick, at Fleming, in Dumfries, and, ultimately sailed from Port Patrick, leaving behind him such an odour of sanctity, that among the most distinguished families of the Scottish aristocracy, Patrick has been a favorite name down to the present day. Arriving in England he preached in Patterdale, (Patrick's dale) in Westmorland, and founded the church of Kirkpatrick, in Durham. Visiting Wales he walked over Sarn-Badrig,

(Patrick's causeway) which, now covered by the sea, forms a dangerous shoal in Carnarvon Bay; and, departing for the Continent, sailed from Llan-Badrig, (the Church of Patrick,) in the island of Anglesea. Undertaking his mission to convert the Irish, he first landed at Innish-Patrick, (the island of Patrick,) and next at Holm Patrick, on the opposite shore of the main land, in the county of Dublin. Sailing northwards he touched at the Isle of Man, some times since also called Innis-Patrick, where he founded another church of Kirk-Patrick, near the town of Peel. Again, landing at the coast of Ireland, in the county of Down, he converted and baptized the chieftain Dicha, on his own threshing floor. The name of the parish of Saul, derived from Sabhal-Patrick, (the barn of Patrick), perpetuates the event. He then proceeded to Temple-Patrick, in Antrim, and from thence to a lofty mountain in Mayo, ever since called Croagh Patrick.

He founded an abbey in East Meath, called Domnach-Padraig, (the house of Patrick,) and built a church in Dublin on the spot where St. Patrick's Cathedral now stands. In an island of Lough Derg, in the county of Donegal, there is St. Patrick's Purgatory; in Leinster, St. Patrick's Wood; at Cashel, St. Patrick's Rock; the St. Patrick's Wells, at which the holy man is said to have quenched his thirst, may be counted by dozens. He is commonly stated to have died at Saul, on the 17th day of March, 493, in the 121st year of his age."

Before examining the question, I was inclined to believe that St. Patrick had been born in Brittany. Dr. Lanigan's demonstration, repeated in Mr. Hoey's essay, first prevented me from adopting that erroneous opinion. Their arguments in favour of Boulogne, for the reasons I have specified, failed to satisfy my judgment. They, however, stimulated my curiosity, and caused me to investigate. The result of my enquiries is the conclusion that their assertions about the

C

birth place of St. Patrick are unsupported by evidence, and erroneous. The modern French theory adopted by these learned gentlemen is not more tenable than the somewhat older one they have themselves refuted; and nothing is gained to historic truth by the substitution of one delusion for another.

Although Dr. Rock, in 1844, had already pointed out the inconsistencies of Lanigan's assertions, and satisfactorily answered the question—Where was St. Patrick born? yet, as Mr. Hoey has endeavoured to infuse new life into the exploded theory, and to enforce it by additional arguments or illustrations—a repetition, and if possible a farther elucidation of the truth has become expedient. I will now endeavour to supply this desideratum.

Of the different localities assigned, of course one only could have been the birth place of St. Patrick. As I was not present on that auspicious occasion, any more than Dr. Lanigan or Mr. Hoey, I must, in looking for it, be guided by the oldest and the best authorities. I cannot, like them, *not only without, but clearly against all ancient authority*, by the mere spelling of a word, solve so intricate a question; yet, such spelling may possibly assist me to the better understanding of the authors who have treated of the subject.

Although Dr. Lanigan modestly informs us in his preface that by him " the mistakes of Colgan, Usher, Ware, and still more of Harris, together with the numberless errors of our monasticons, have been carefully corrected;" and Mr. Hoey, while adopting his theory, pronounces Lanigan " the most acute, the most conscientious, and perhaps the most generally learned of Irish historians;" yet, I cannot justly be accused of presumption for declining to be guided by their bare or ill-supported assertions on a point on which they are contradicted by others at least as acute, conscientious, and learned, as themselves. They are contradicted by Matthew of Westminster, commonly called Florilegus, and by Cardinal Baronius, who say that St. Patrick was an Irishman—" Natione

Hibernensi ;" by Don Philip O'Sullivan, and by the corrector (though in this case the corruptor) of the Breviary of Rouen, who maintain that he was a native of Brittany; by Mr Lynch, and the Rev. P. McLachlan of Stirling, who believe that he was born in France, in the city of Tours; by Marianus Scotus, and William of Malmsbury; by the old and present Roman Breviaries; by that of St. John Lateran; by those of Paris, Rheims, and Armagh, which say that he was a native of Britain; by Sigibert de Gemblours, and by the the martyrologies of Bede, Usuard, Rabanus, and Ado, which call him a Scot—" xvi. Kal. April, in Scotia natale S. Patricii ;"—by Buchanan, Hollinshead, Pinkerton, and the Rev. Thomas Innes, who maintain that he was born at Kilpatrick, on the Clyde, between Dumbarton and Glasgow. Father Innes, in confirmation of his assertion, refers to Usher, Ware, Colgan, Flaherty, Cave, the Bollandists, Mabillon, Tillemont, and Bailet. The same is affirmed by the Abbe MacGeoghegan in his History of Ireland; by Reeves and Alban Butler; by Drs. Todd, Rock, O'Connor, O'Donovan, and O'Curry.

As Mr. Hoey admits that the weight of authority is clearly against Boulogne, and in favour of Kilpatrick, I need not enter very deeply into this portion of the subject. Indeed, my main object is to exhibit the concord of the old authorities, and to resume the enterprise abandoned by him, of pointing out, in the vicinity of Dumbarton, the localities mentioned in St. Patrick's Confession. In estimating the value of the authorities to which I have to refer, I must unquestionably assign the first place to the writings of St. Patrick, viz.:—his Confession and his Letter to Coroticus.

You have already learned from his Confession that he was born at Bonaven Taberniæ, or at the mouth of a river flowing into the Irish Sea. When to this I add another extract in which he styles Britain his fatherland, you will have the best possible proof, St. Patrick's own words, of his British origin, (29) "Ut, &c." "That going to Britain, as to my native

country, and to my parents, and I was most heartily disposed
(to do so); not only that, but (to proceed) even unto Gaul
to visit the brethren, and that I might see the face of the
saints of my Lord." The Latin word Britannias leaves here
no room for mistakes or confusion of ideas. Had the saint
called his country simply Britannia, that would still have
meant Great Britain. Whenever any other place is called
Britannia, it is always qualified by an epithet which distin-
guishes it from Great Britain, such as Britannia Minor, Britannia Gallicana. The word in the plural number is intelligible only of this Britain, divided by the Romans into Britannia Prima, Britannia Secunda, Flavia Cæsariensis, Maxima
Cæsariensis, (30) and still more effectually by Hadrian's
wall, extending from the Tyne to the Solway, as well as by
that of Antoninus from the Clyde to the Forth, which made
it like separate islands. (31)

Dr. Rock has explained this point far better than I can.

" From those two short writings—the Confession, (32) and
the Letter to Coroticus, (33) deemed by the ablest critics to
be the genuine production of Ireland's apostle, we gather
that St. Patrick himself reckoned the insular Britons his
countrymen, called Britain his native land, and looked upon
it as his home and the dwelling-place of his kindred; distin-
guishing it very broadly from Gaul, or modern France. For
otherwise, how could St. Patrick, in a letter to a British prince
—for such was Coroticus—have called that chief's subjects
his fellow-citizens, and distinguished them from the Romans
settled in Britain, if he were not well known to the world to
be a born Briton? or how could he, with any truth, apply to
his own person that saying of holy writ—" A prophet is not
without honour save in his own country and in his own
house," (S. Matt. xiii, 57) unless Coroticus and everyone else
were fully aware that Britain was the holy man's birth-place.

Although I have but little faith in poets, and require historical facts to be attested by more reliable evidence than

their effusions; yet so much is made of St. Feich's hymn, both by Dr. Lanigan and Mr. Hoey, that I here quote Dr. Rock's observations on the import of that document.

" Not long after the death of St. Patrick, was written in his honour the hymn which goes under Feich's name; but, whoever wrote it, as well as its very ancient commentator, assign the British city of Alcluith, under the poetical name of Nemthur (34) as the birthplace of the Saint; and, glancing at his travels on the Continent, point out Armorica as a land which he had to reach by sea, which could not be true, nor would have been so noticed in the Hymn, had St. Patrick been born in any part of Gaul."

From the life ascribed to St. Evin, (36) we learn that St. Patrick was of the Britons of Strathclyde; or, as he has it, Alclyde, and born in Nempthur. " De Britannis Alcluiden-sibus, (37) natus in Nempthur."

To the same purpose we have the concurrent testimony of all the other lives of St. Patrick, and of all the Breviaries cited by Mr. Hoey, with the single exception of the corrected Breviary of Rouen. Although some of those Breviaries say, only in general, that the Saint was born in Britain, while others mention the particular locality, yet there is no contradiction or any real difference between them. (38) Thus, the Roman Breviaries tell us that he was " by race a Briton " and born " in the great island of Britain," " in the Greater Britain;" that of Rheims—" in the maritime territory of Britain;" those of Paris and Armagh—in Britain, in the fortified town of Emptor, or Emphthoria. The lives attributed to SS. Patrick Junior, Benignus, and Eleran, give the honour of his birth to the fortified town Nempthur—in the field of Tab-urnia. To these authorities, Mr. Hoey adds passages from Probus and Jocelin, which require to be considered more in detail. According to Jocelin, St. Patrick's father—Cal-purnius, a Briton in the district of Taburnia—so called from the fact of the Romans having there fixed their tents, resided near Nempthor, by the Irish Sea. The Saint's mother was a native of France, and clandestinely or forcibly brought to North Britain; and St. Patrick was reared at Nempthor. He, also, refers to Dumbarton, describing it as a certain fort, of which the ruins were visible in his days, situated on a promontory higher than the fortified town Nempthor. (40)

We have the same fact narrated in the First Lesson, on the 17th of March, in the Aberdeen Breviary, (41) where it is stated that St. Patrick's father, Calpurnius, was of a noble Scottish family, and his mother, Conchessa, sister to St. Martin, Bishop of Tours; and that he (St. Patrick) was ominously begotten in the castle of Dumbarton, and born and educated in Kilpatrick, near the same castle, in Scotland. That at baptism he was called Suthat; afterwards, by St. Germanus, Magonius; and Patricius or Patrick, by Pope Celestine. (42)

Having, in the first part of this dissertation, related the statement of Probus (43) on this subject, I have now laid before you the most ancient records relative to the birth-place of St. Patrick; and I wish you to observe that not even one of them maintains his having been born in any part of France, or anywhere out of Scotland. The expression in the Breviary of Rouen, "in Britannia Gallicana," as Dr. Lanigan admits, is attributable to its corrector or corruptor. The theory of the Saint's having been born at Boulogne is quite a late invention, for fourteen hundred years after his nativity unheard of.

In order that the testimony of these authorities may be better understood and appreciated, I must now call attention to the change that has come over the general aspect of the country, in the lapse of time, by the vicissitudes of conquest and of successive colonization; and, still more, by modern enterprise, and the operations of pastoral, agricultural, and commercial improvements. In the year of our Lord eighty-one, the Roman general, Agricola, having invaded and subjugated the Lowland portion of Scotland, erected a line of forts from Cairiden, on the Forth, to Old Kilpatrick, on the Clyde. In 140, Lollius Urbicus, Proprætor of Britain under the Emperor Antoninus, constructed, on the line of Agricola's forts, a *prætentura*, consisting first of a ditch twenty feet deep and forty feet wide (which could probably be filled with water when required); secondly, of a rampart twenty feet high and forty-two feet thick, composed of earth, on a stone foundation, 36 miles and 620 yards in length, and fortified by nineteen forts, placed at intervals of about two miles, exclusive of the stations at each extremity; thirdly, of a military road within the rampart, from end to end, as a necessary means of communication between the forts and stations. He, also, built a fort at Dun Glass. Again, in 370, this prætentura was repaired by Theodosius, under Valentinian. Theodosius erected the territory between this wall of Antoninus and that of Hadrian, into a province, which he called Valentia, in honor of the emperor. He extended the Roman forts to Dumbarton, which he built, and to which he gave the name of Theodosia, and made it the capital of the province. The wall was subsequently repaired and strengthened by additional fortifications, by Stilicho, in 398, and finally by the Britons in 409. No doubt those latter fortifications consisted of the smaller castles, turrets, and watch-towers mentioned by Roy in his Military Antiquities, p. 156. Opposite the Roman wall there were nine Caledonian Hill-forts, besides three somewhat farther off, near the Carron. The remains of these fortifications were to be seen for many ages, though gradually disappearing, and some traces of them may yet be seen in several places along the line. In 1686, the Roman forts were distinctly and accurately traced by Dr. Irvine. At the west end, referred to by Jocelin, Dr. Irvine found (1) at Dumbarton, a great fort; (2) the castle half a mile from it; (3) a mile thence, at the foot of Dumbuck Hill, a fort; (4) a mile thence, at Dunglass, a fort; (5) a mile thence to Chapel Hill, above the town of Kilpatrick, a fort, &c. They have been since surveyed by Gordon, Horsley, and Roy. There was but one military station at the East end of the wall at Cairiden, but there were three at the west—one at Kilpatrick, one at Dunglass, and one at Dumbarton. These were necessary to protect the Roman anchorages at Dumbarton and Dunglass, and also to prevent the enemy from passing into the Roman territory, by the Clyde, which could then be forded even as low as Dunbuck. At Kilpatrick, within the prætentura, was the western market town, or Emporium, of the Romans for a long time, indeed till Theodosia was built. After it was made a province, Valentia remained but for a short time, (forty years), in the possession of the Romans. Theodosia lost its Latin name, and under that of Alcluith, or Alclyde, became the capital of the British kingdom of Strath Clyde. The wall was not always, if at any time, the exact boundary of the Roman dominion, and it had to be frequently repaired, on account of the constant incursions of the barbarians. Almost as soon as Agricola had retreated, after the battle of the Grampians, the vanquished tribes recovered their liberty, and with the unsubdued Caledonians, so molested the Roman provinces that to check their inroads,

In 120, the wall of Hadrian was built.

  „ 139, a general revolt.

  „ 140, Lollius Urbicus built the Wall of Antoninus.

  „ 161, invasion and disturbances, quelled by Calpurnius Agricola.

  „ 183, new incursions, Mæatæ subdued.

  „ 200, treaty with the Lieutenant of Severus.

  „ 207, new hostilities.

  „ 209, Severus lost 50,000 men, principally in contending with the natural difficulties of the country.

  „ 210, the South Wall rebuilt.

In 212, peace with Caracalla, after the battle of Carron.

,, 343, incursions mentioned on doubtful authority.

,, 360, the Picts and Scots invade.

,, 364, attacks by Picts, Scots, Attacotts, and Saxons.

,, 369, repulsed by Theodosius.

,, 370, Valentia established.

,, 398, invasion by Picts and Scots repulsed with assistance from Stilicho.

,, 408; the Britons form for themselves an independent government, and ask assistance from the Romans.

,, 422, the Britons repel the invaders, with the assistance of the Romans, and re-build the Wall for the last time,

when, as Bede informs us, the Irish returned home, and the Picts settled down for the first time in the extremity of the Island; occasionally, however, plundering the territories of the Britons. (44)

More than one genealogy has been devised for St Patrick, (45) which, however, the Bollandists justly consider unworthy of investigation. His father's name, Calpurnius, suggests the probability of his descent from Calpurnius Agricola, who was sent to command in this part of Britain, A.D. 161, as we learn from Capitolinus. This would also account for the name by which he is universally known (Patricius), though his baptismal name was Succath: as the magistrates in the provinces were called Patricians, like the senators at Rome. This title is said to have been conferred upon him by Pope Celestine, on occasion of his receiving the apostolical benediction and his mission from that Pontiff. But I cannot learn clearly from history that, at so early a period, the Pope had the power of conferring civil dignities and titles: and Alban Butler remarks, in his Life of St. Patrick, that " it seems, from his Confession, that he was ordained deacon, priest, and bishop for his mission in his own country." I know not if

Calpurnius Agricola was a Christian; he might have been so, or his descendants might have been such. Certain it is that, in the time of St. Patrick, there was in Britain a Christian, possibly his relation, by name Agricola, an active disseminator of Pelagianism. This circumstance most likely suggested to St. Patrick the propriety of framing for the Church he established in Ireland the canon, which explicitly requires that all matters of difficulty and intricacy that could not readily be decided by the primate and his council should be referred to the Holy See.

St. Patrick's Roman provincial origin is not disputed, and yet the evidence thereof (his father's name and office, and the cited portion of his Letter to Coroticus) is not so clear as that which shows him to have been a native of Great Britain. Save his own words, already quoted, nothing could better demonstrate the country he belonged to than the term *Brito*, applied to him by Probus, Jocelin, and the old Roman Breviary. We learn the meaning of this word from the *Acta Sanctorum*, l. xii. p. 535, where we are told that the Romans separated, first by the Wall of Adrian, and, secondly, by that of Severus, the Britons whom they had conquered, from those they could not overcome; who, in Latin, from the fact were called Picti, (*i.e.* painted, according to the signification of the ancient name Brith), because they stained their bodies with an azure or ultramarine colour. (46) Here it is also mentioned that the wall was built from the (Irish) sea to the river Forth on the (German) ocean, to keep the enemies (the Picts and Scots) from the Britons. (47) "A Britonibus." The root of the term Brito is the Celtic word Bri, *i.e.*, substance, whence comes the Gælic word Brigh, (*pr.* Bri), juice, and the Lowland Scotch Bree; and also Brit, Brith—spotted. I find likewise in the Gælic dictionaries Briot, (Brit) which we now express by the term Breac (Brec). We use the same word to signify a trout, which is also spotted, but in the plural and oblique cases, Bric. Thus we are enabled to account for the different forms of the word Briton already enumerated. From Brith, or Brit, are formed Brito, Briton, Britan, Britain, Britti, Brytta, Bryttar, Bret, Breton; and from Breac—Bracti. (48) The subdued and civilized Britons discontinued the practice of staining their persons while they retained the name Britones, and distinguished the unconquered Caledonian tribes by the name Picti. The taste for variegated colours is to this day manifested in their descendants by the variously coloured checks of the Highland tartans.

On Pinkerton's Map of Britain at the time of its abandonment by the Romans, (in the days of St. Patrick), the Britones are placed to the south of the wall between the Forth and Clyde.

Next to Brito, the words Tabernia and Emptor or Nemptor require our attention.

Mr. Hoey asserts that there is no appearance of certainty in the minds of the principal authorities for the history of St. Patrick as to the exact site of the places of which they speak when they mention Empthoria, or Nemthur, and Tabernia, as he says, none of them venture to name the exact district or diocese in which they are to be found. Such, however, is not the case.

The Bonaven Taberniæ in St. Patrick's Confession must, when he wrote in the middle of the fifth century, and for some time thereafter, have been common and well known names of the places to which he applied them; as they are the only words he found it necessary to use in order to be understood. When, through the lapse of time, the transmigration of peoples, and the altered state of the country, those names were changed, and in danger of being forgotten or not understood, we are directed by his biographers in the sixth and seventh centuries, to the Britons of Strath-Clyde. The fact is that the Britons assailed from the south by the Saxons, and from the west by the Irish, the Scots, and the Picts, crowded into Valentia,

between the walls, and organised a government for themselves. From the time that they repulsed the Scots and
Picts (A.D. 422) and rebuilt the wall their capital was
called Alcluyd, Dunclyd, and Dunbriton.

According to the Annals of Ulster, Alclyde was besieged
for four months, and destroyed by the Norwegians and
Danes from Ireland, under Olave and Ivar, in 872. Bromp-
ton assigns its destruction by the Danes to the year 869. In
875, the Vikingr, sailing from Northumberland, wasted
Galloway and Strath-Clyde. In 890, many of the Strath-
clyde Britons emigrated to Wales, where the Welsh king,
Anarawd, then hard pressed by the Saxons, assigned them
a district which they were to acquire by their valour and
defend by their policy. " This generous condition they performed by assisting the Welsh to defeat the Saxons in the
battle of Cymrid, and to drive the odious intruders from the
disputed land. The descendants of the Strathclydensian
emigrants remain a distinguishable people in North Wales
even to this day. Strathclyde was for ever annexed to the
Scottish crown by the successful efforts of Kenneth III." (49)
(Chalmers' Caledonia, v. i, p. 355-7) From that time Dunbriton
was called by the Scoto-Irish Dunbreatann (*pr.* Dunbretun).

The words used by St. Evin, "De Britannis Alcluidensibus,"
i.e. of the Britons of Alclyde, are not necessarily restricted to
the capital Alclyd, for it was not an uncommon practice in
the middle ages to name kingdoms by their capitals. (50) St.
Evin's assertion is supported by the concurrent testimony of
St. Eleran, who says the Saint's parents were "De Strato
Cluidi," *i. e.* from or of Strathclyde, and both maintain that
he was born in Nempthur of Taburnia.

As the kingdom of Strathclyde was not very large,
comprising only, according to Pinkerton, Renfrew, Dumbarton, and part of Lanarkshire, from the year 426, when
the Picts seized the eastern portion of Valentia down to the
wall of Gallio, the range for enquiry is not very great, being

only eighty miles long by thirty broad, When given, the direction was sufficient, because St. Patrick's birth-place would readily be pointed out by those Britons near whose capital he had been born, who revered him as a saint, and who maintained their position and independence till towards the close of the tenth century. Even yet a part of this description is very clear; and the rest, to some, intelligible. The ancient scholiast on St. Feich's hymn surely had some idea of the locality where Nemthur was to be found, when he wrote that it was a city in North Britain, namely, Al-cluid. (51) So had Jocelin of the situation of both what he calls Taburnia and Nempthor, when he wrote that St. Patrick was a North-Briton and born in the district of Taburnia, near Nempthor, by the Irish Sea. This very knowledge of the place, together with his ignorance of the Celtic, caused him to misinterpret the word Tabernia into "Tabernaculorum campus," or the field of tents or stations, which he plainly tells us were erected by the Romans. So well did he know the ground that he mentions the remains of a fort on a promontory higher than Nempthor to be seen even in his days. A more accurate description of the locality could not easily be given. Even Dr. Lanigan dared not deny that Jocelin had a very definite idea of the position of Nempthor and Tabernia, and Mr. Hoey admits that Colgan quotes Jocelin as his authority for placing Tabernia on the south bank of the Clyde.

A similar knowledge of the locality, along with such a loose acceptation of St. Feich's words as we have from Dr. O'Connor (*Natus* instead of *genitus* est Patricius Nemturri), seems to have led others to interpret Nempthur by Heavenly or Holy Tower. For the mound on which stood the Roman station above Kilpatrick, near the end of the wall of Antoninus, is still called Chapel-hill, sufficiently indicating that a church or chapel had there succeeded the station.

Probus, a more ancient writer than Jocelin, having

flourished in the ninth century, is not less explicit, although he has been misunderstood. According to him, as already mentioned, St. Patrick was a Briton and born in the village Bannave, in the district of Tiburnia, not far from the western sea. So far in his peculiar dialect he adheres to the words of the Confession and consequently must be right. To show, however, that he knew and wished to let others know where Bonaven Taberniæ was situated, he adds: " We have found unquestionably that this village is in the province of Nevtria or Neutria, where the giants are said to have dwelt. I find this word written Neutria by Dr. Rock, (who quotes Probus, *in Vita* S. Patricii, *inter opera* Bedæ;) Nentria by the Bollandists, who say Probus ought and wished to have written Nemthuria; and Nevtria by Dr. Lanigan. Anciently *v* and *u* were but one letter, which was read according to its import. I have already explained the orthography of Nemtur or Neutria. Now, supposing the Bollandists are right, and that the proper form of the word, as set down by Probus, was Nentria for Nenturia—the Celtic Nemtùr—the province Nentria would mean *the province or district of the towers*. That such was Probus's meaning is put beyond all doubt by what follows—" Where the giants are said to have dwelt."

Who were the giants, and where did they reside? Finan Mac Con is mentioned by Jocelin as a giant who lived a hundred years before St. Patrick. There is no reason to doubt that Probus also meant the same Fionn McChomhail, or as McPherson renders it, Fingal and his associates, the heroes of Ossian's Poems. (52) Although they are styled only heroes by the bards, they are spoken of as giants by the vulgar. Hector Boetius also describes Fionn as of a gigantic size, and makes him fifteen cubits high. The testimony of the bards is supported by a tradition still alive, and chronicled by our historians, which assures us that Fionn and his hosts contended against the Romans on the banks of the Carron; and, likewise, by the evidence deducible from the names of the places occupied by the Fingalians or Finnians to the west of the wall of Antoninus. In the Campsie hills, near Lachie Burn, a tributary to the Carron, there is Dnn-Goil, *i.e.*, the hill of Goll or Gaul (the son of Morni, one of Fionn's generals), and also Fin-Glen and Ossian Hill, which some Saxon surveyor has written Owsen Hill on the map No. 30 of the Ordnance Survey of Scotland. On the Endrick there is Fintry, seemingly a corruption of Fion-triath, (*gen.*, treith), which means the chieftain Finn; farther to the west is Finary, *i.e.*, Finn's field, or, according to the present acceptance of the word Airidh, (*pronounced* ari,) Finn's summer residence. At Dumbarton Muir, or rather among the hills of Kilpatrick, there is Fyn Loch and Fin Loch Hill. A mile from Loch Lomond, on the road due west from Arden, may be seen Dun-Fin (the primary meaning of Dun is a hill; its secondary meaning, a fortress); and, immediately above it, Meikle Dunfin—Finn's great fort. Still further westward we find Loch Goil, *i.e.*, the loch of Goll (loch means either a lake or a portion of the sea running into the land); and Loch-Fyn, now Loch-Fyne; and also Cowal, the Covalia of Buchanan and Camden, in Gælic orthography Comhal, Finn's father, from whom that country has its name. (53) That the Scots and Picts here successfully resisted the Roman arms is a fact too well known and established by authentic history, to admit of contradiction. And thus our tradition and our poetry seem in this instance as credible as the statements of the Roman panegyrists, who could well afford to record the loss of a battle, but not the succession of calamitous defeats implied by the victories of the Finnians, and the loss by Severus during his campaign in North Britain of 50,000 men. Such a disaster is not sufficiently accounted for by the rigours of the climate, and the roughness of the country. (54) Judging of the Finnians by the time of their exploits, and their topographical position, they are the Atta-

cotti mentioned somewhat later by Ammianus Marcellinus.
Indeed, their name implies as much. (55) If the elucidation
of my subject depended upon the probability of my inducing
all to yield assent to these arguments and illustrations, I
should much fear that, after all my diligent researches, my
labours would prove unsuccessful. Happily, however, for
the cause of truth, so much is not required. The authen-
ticity of Ossian's poems, the truth or falsehood of the history
of the Finnians, their Scotch or Irish origin is of no consequence to my purpose. It is enough that they are said to
have dwelt near the wall of Antoninus, in the district of the
towers, so that the words of Probus—"Quem vicum (Bonaven) indubitanter comperimus esse Nentriæ provinciæ, in qua
olim gigantes habitasse dicuntur"—become perfectly intelligible in the sense of the author. Probus is not then, as
would appear to superficial observers, at variance with St.
Evin the scholiast, and the other authorities I have quoted;
but, as is evident by his expression, "Nentriæ provinciæ,"
having already mentioned Bannave Tyburniæ, takes a wider
range, in order to demonstrate unmistakeably the district,
or *province*, as he calls it, containing the birth-place of
St. Patrick. I must now examine another passage from this
same author, in which he calls Bonaven Taberniæ by a different name, and which has been misunderstood by Dr. Lanigan and others.

Speaking of St. Patrick, Probus says—"Whilst yet he was
in his own country with his father, Calpurnius, and his mother Conchessa, with his brother Ructis, and his sister, by
name Mila, in their city Arimuric, a great sedition took place
in those parts, for the sons of the British king Rethmitus
were laying waste Arimuric." (56)

I confess this to be a difficult passage, requiring an inti-
mate acquaintance with the locality mentioned, and the language in which the sense is involved. Yet, when well

studied, and properly understood, it is quite explicit and conclusive.

Considering the text, we perceive by the word *sedition*, that the natives of the country were engaged in the assault on Arimuric; and, also, that the attack was made under the direction, or at any rate with the co-operation of the sons of a British king. There were no kings in Britain at the time of St. Patrick's captivity, except beyond the northern wall; all the rest of Britain being then subject to the Romans. We are well assured by Roman writers that the unconquered tribes made frequent incursions into the province of Valentia, and also that in some of these plundering expeditions, they were aided by the Irish. (57) Thus, we know that Rethmitus was a Scottish king, yet where in Scotland this king reigned is not so easily determined. First, because we have not separate and complete lists of the kings who ruled the different tribes into which the Caledonians were divided, viz. Vecturiones, Mæatæ, Dicalidones, Attacotti, Horesti, Scoti, and Dalreudini, or Dalriads. (58) Secondly, for want of a complete history of the country at the period in question. The little we know of it, with certainty, we learn from a few passages to be met with in the writings of Roman authors. Thirdly, by reason of our often finding, in old writings, proper names so variously spelt, that it is with difficulty we can recognise the names of well-known kings, or other persons. Thus, the sixty-second on the list of Pictish kings is written in the Chronicon Pictorum, *Nechthon ;* in the registry of St. Andrew's, *Nectan;* by Fordun, *Nectane;* by Winton, *Nactan;* by the Irish Nennius, *Nectonus;* in Tighernach, *Netan.* So, also, Canut the thirty-third, in the same line, is written in the Chronicon Pictorum, *Ulachama*; in Reg. St. And., *Canatulmel;* by Fordun, *Canatulmel;* by Winton, *Enalculmel.* In like manner, Sedulius, according to Colgan, is rendered in Irish Seidhuil. Thus, also, the Abbe Mac Geoghegan writes in his History of Ireland Seaghlin for Secundinus, and

Tomultach O'Connor, for Thomas O'Connor, Archbishop of Ardmach. Hence arises my inability to give any farther certain account of Rethmitus. When I consider the time of the sack of Arimuric, as indicated by the presence there of St. Patrick's father, Calpurnius, I am inclined to think that Probus meant the sons of Cairbre Riada, an Irish chieftain, who settled with his followers in Kintyre, for some time called Dalriada, in the beginning of the third century, and by English and Irish writers generally supposed to be the same as Eocha Riata, or Rieta, also Reuther (from whom Rutherglen derives its name), mentioned in the series of Scottish kings. When I look to the text and take into account the reference made to the Finnians, or Fingalians, and observe the name (Rethmitus), I am more disposed to believe that Probus meant the sons or descendants of Reuthámir, a king of Balclutha, (59) mentioned in one of Ossian's poems entitled " Carthon."

In order to understand Probus and the other writers who have mentioned St. Patrick's birth-place, we must bear in mind that this portion of the country has been successively occupied by the Britons, the Romans, the Picts, Attacots, Scots, Irish, and promiscuously by Saxons, Danes, and Normans; and that, consequently, the names of the various localities have been more or less changed and affected by the different languages spoken by those several races. At first the names of places were merely generic, very few having specific names, and those generally descriptive. We must understand this text consistently with what we have already learned from Probus—viz., that St. Patrick was a Briton, and born in Britain, in Bannave, Tyburniæ, not far from the western sea, in the district of Nentria, *of the towers*, i.e., near the wall of Antoninus. If, then, you ask me where was the town called Arimuric, I answer at Kilpatrick. The name is not yet lost, although somewhat changed by the Scandinavian successors of the Celtic population. The field on the west end of which

Kilpatrick stands is still called Dalmuir, which has the same meaning as Àiridhmhuir (pronounced Arivuir), *i. e.*, the field of the wall. It is distinctly marked on the Ordnance Survey Map, No. 30. The next station to the east of Kilpatrick on the line of railway between Glasgow and Dumbarton is called Dalmuir. Arimuric is composed of two Gælic words— Àiridh and Mùr. The first I have already explained; the second means a wall. (60)

Now let us look for Em-tur, Emptor, Nempthor, Nemthor, Nemeton, Nempthur, or Empthoria.

Should Mr. Hoey be satisfied with the similarity of names and the proximity to a Roman station, without going to France, I would direct his attention to a village called Nemphlar, distant two miles from Lanark; or, should he insist on a place denominated " The tower," I would leave him to choose between the Torr, a little to the north of Helensburgh, and the Dun, at Bowling, a mile from Old Kilpatrick. Tower and Dun are in a sense synonimous; for though the primary signification of Dun is an elevation or hill, its secondary meaning is a fortress or castle. Duns are as plenty in Scotland as towers in Ireland. We have at least three scores of places called Dun, or into whose names Dun enters as a component part. The summit of the Dun at Bowling is rendered almost inaccessible by precipitous rocks on three sides—on the fourth; the south, I observed some faint traces of roads and walls, which led me to the conclusion that it had once been used as a place of defence, or more probably of observation.

Against the two first places there are strong objections. Nemphlar seems to be a contraction and corruption of Knights-Templars, who anciently had a chapel at the village, and it is not at the mouth of a river, nor yet near the western or the Irish sea. Torr is considerably beyond the limits of the Roman province Valentia, while it is clear that St. Patrick was a Roman Briton.

St. Feich's Em-tur may signify the castle of Dumbarton, in which there was anciently a chapel dedicated to St. Patrick, (61) and thus it would agree with the Aberdeen Breviary; or it may mean the Dun, if it had a tower, or any of the forts along the wall of Antoninus; but most probably it refers to Chapel-hill. I say most probably Chapel-hill by reason of the interpretation given by St. Feich's scholiast and others to the name, viz., Holy Tower. Secondly, because tradition and the name assure us that on the site of the Roman station there stood a chapel. (This church also might have had a tower). Thirdly, because a church on Chapel-hill, so near to that in the village of Kilpatrick, was not, as far as we can learn, at any time required to accommodate the population of the village, and must therefore have been built, most likely, according to the Catholic practice, out of reverence for, and in commemoration of the supernatural manifestations mentioned in the office of the Church on occasion of St. Patrick's conception in the fortress. Fourthly, because it is not certain that there was a tower on the Dun. Fifthly, because according to the most ancient biographies of St. Patrick, he was born before the erection, in 369, of Dumbarton Castle, and Theodosia, subsequently called Alcluith, Alcluyd, Dunclud, Dunbritton, Dunbreatann, Dunbertan, Dunbarton, Dumbarton. (62) All this, however, bears but indirectly on the subject of my investigation, as it relates only to the place of St. Patrick's conception, not of his nativity. Reverting then from this digression, to the sole object of my enquiry, I ask where is Nempthor, near which Jocelin, SS. Evin, Eleran, Benignus, and Patrick Junior, St. Feich's commentator, and the Breviaries of Paris and Armagh say St. Patrick was born. For the reasons already assigned it must be at or near Kilpatrick. The Annals of Ulster, which change Alcluith into Alocluathe, mention a rock called Mimro, which may possibly be an Irish name for Nempthor. This Mimro seems to have

been the Rock of Dumbarton, since the Annals tell us
that a battle was fought at a rock called Mimro by the
Dalriads, or Irish of Argyle, and the Britons of Strath-
clyde, A.D. 716. The word, however, is so much changed
that nothing definite can be inferred from it. Dr. Lanigan
denied the existence of Nempthor in Britain, because he had
not found it mentioned in Nennius's list of British towns, nor
in any of the old Itineraries, nor in Ricardus Corenensis, nor
in Camden, Horsley, &c. Their silence would, at the most,
establish only a presumption, not a proof, of its non-existence.
The breviaries of Armagh and Paris tell us expressly that
Emptor or Empthoria was in Britain, and we have seen that
St. Fiech's commentator places it in North Britain at Alcluith.
If the Doctor had examined Horsley's Britannia Romana minutely, he might have recognised it in Nemeton among the
towns he assigns to Scotland, from those mentioned by the
anonymous geographer of Ravenna. (63) The geographer
marks the situation of Nemeton by stating that it is where
Britain is narrowest from sea to sea, and that it, and the
other towns mentioned, are connected with one another.
From this description the towns named were evidently along
the wall of Antoninus, between the Clyde and Forth; and
this, together with Jocelin's statement that Nempthor was in
North Britain ("oppidum"), a fortified or walled town, close
to the Irish sea, in a lower situation than the other fort on a
promontory (Dumbarton), of which the ruins were visible
in his time, enables us to say definitely that it was the Roman
station on Chapel-hill. The geographer of Ravenna having
written in most barbarous Latin, the difference in the spelling
of the word is easily conceived. He has corrupted, in the
same way, the names of several other well-known towns,
some of them into a kind of Italian—thus he has changed
the Uxellum of Ptolomy into Uxelia, Lucopidia into Luco-
tion, Corda into Coria, and Trimontium into Trimuntium.
Even more accurate authors do not all write this word in the

same way. Jocelin has it Nempthor or Nemthor; Dr. Lanigan makes it Emtor; the lives ascribed to SS. Evin, Patrick Junior, Benignus, and Eleran—Nempthur; the Breviary of Armagh—Emptor; and that of Paris—Empthoria. In all these forms it is not Celtic, because there is no word in Gælic beginning with either Nemp or Emp: it is barbarous Latin—a proper name made of a common noun. It has evidently acquired the letter N, like St. Feich's Nemtur, from the preposition in, (64) and Emptor and Empthoria are easily detected as barbarous phonetic corruptions of the Latin word Emporium, a market-town. To comprehend how the word became thus corrupted requires but little thought. When the Romans and their market had disappeared from the scene, the proper form and the import of the word Emporium, which the uncivilized Scotch and Irish had undoubtedly heard, was lost; but, as the towers remained, and they knew of the miraculous conception of St Patrick in a tower, and that a chapel had been built in his honour on the site of the fort, the tor of Emptor seems to have been taken for a word signifying a tower, instead of a mere Latin termination, and was converted by the Irish, according to the idiom of their language, into túr and thúr. That such was the case appears from the Irish explanation of the term, viz., heavenly tower, and the retention of the p in Nempthur, as well as in Emptor and Empthoria. The p, preserved in all the oldest forms of the word, is a conclusive proof not merely against its fancied Celtic, but likewise a clear indication of its real Latin origin Emporium, which comes itself from *Emptor*, a buyer.

We have now ten words which express the birth-place of St. Patrick, which may be reduced to four intelligible names: 1. Bonaven Tabernæ; or Probus's version of it—Bannave Tyburniæ. 2. The six corruptions of Emporium. 3. Arimuric. 4. Kilpatrick. All these names are successively applicable to Kilpatrick, but to no other place. 1. It is at the mouth of a river falling into the Irish Sea. 2. It was an emporium

of the Romans. 3. It was the field of the wall (of Antoninus). 4. Of the six parishes under his patronage in the
ancient diocese of Glasgow, it was emphatically the Church
of St. Patrick, dedicated in his honour to God, and erected
on the very spot at which he had been baptised, and the
resort of pious pilgrims during the middle ages. (65) Nempthor is called an *oppidum*, or walled or fortified town, by
Jocelin, by three other biographers of St. Patrick, and two
of the Breviaries; and is said by the geographer of Ravenna to have been joined to other towns between the Clyde
and Forth; and therefore I conclude its situation to have been
not where the village of Kilpatrick now stands, but beside it
on Chapel-hill, where our antiquarians are now agreed, from
the discoveries made there of sepulchral stones, coins, and other
Roman remains, besides other reasons, that there was not only
a fort, but a station for troops, and the end of the wall of
Antoninus.

When Jocelin says that the Saint was born not in, but
near (secus) the fortified town or station Nempthor, he agrees
perfectly with Probus and thé Aberdeen Breviary. The
authors of the other lives, who say "in oppido Nempthur,"
may have used the word in a wider sense, so as to include
the suburbs; or may not have known the ground so well.
Kilpatrick lies contiguous to Chapel-hill, the farthest point
of that plateau not being over a quarter of a mile from the
west end of Kilpatrick.

To this historical, geographical, and etymological evidence
(the latter deduced not merely from one, but from all the
appellations that have been given to the birth-place of Saint
Patrick) must be added the constant and well-sustained tradition of the locality, which even for the last three hundred
years has been firmly maintained by the Protestant inhabitants of Kilpatrick. This tradition is mentioned in the first
and second Statistical Account of Scotland; and also by Mr.
John Dillon, in his Paper on St. Patrick, read to the Society

of Scottish Antiquities on the 25th of November, 1816. Having lately visited Kilpatrick, I found it held as firmly as ever by the villagers.

In his Statistical Account (68) Sir John Sinclair mentions a stone with a figure on it, said to represent Saint Patrick, which is still in the church-yard. I observed that the hands of the figure are in an attitude of prayer, a sword by its side, and a dog or pig under its feet. It has no inscription. I saw nothing clearly indicating its relation to St. Patrick, nor can I account for the cause of its being said to represent him, unless it relates to what is said by some authors—of his having been during his first captivity employed in feeding swine; a more probable cause is the remains of a tradition, now lost in the locality, regarding a stone over the well, which was used as an ordeal for perjury during the middle ages. This stone is the only one in the church-yard remarkable for its antiquity, and people may have fixed upon it as the one to which the tradition referred, before it was wholly forgotten.

Another object requiring more particular attention is what is now called the Trees' Well, situated to the south of the west corner of the grave-yard in which the church stands, and separated from it only by the public road from Dumbarton to Glasgow.

Dr. Lanigan, the fourth Life (cap. 3) in Colgan's collection, that called the Tripartite (l. i., c. 4), Jocelin (c. 2), and the Aberdeen Breviary, make mention of a fountain instantaneously produced on occasion of St. Patrick's baptism, over which the original church was built, and to whose waters miraculous effects were ascribed. Thus Gormias, a man blind from his birth, was said to have obtained his sight by the application of the water to his eyes. (69)

Having already ascertained the fact of St. Patrick's birth in Kilpatrick, we can have no difficulty in recognising the Trees' Well, in the immediate vicinity of the present church, as the miraculous fountain mentioned by the authorities referred to. The present church in Kilpatrick, although erected on the site of a more ancient structure, does not cover the Trees' Well. For the diversity of situation of the original church and of that now in use, quite a sufficient reason is to be found in the fact that the Kirk of Scotland views the use of holy wells as superstitious, and the rigorous ordinances enacted at the Reformation against such as should have recourse to them. (70)

. Dr. Lanigan scornfully rejects the claims of Kilpatrick, because those who relate the tradition have mingled with their narrative what he considers ridiculous fables of miracles ascribed to St. Patrick in his childhood, and by reason of the erection of the church over the fountain. As well might he deny that St. Patrick had sisters, merely because it is absurdly recorded by different authors, as he admits, that they followed the Saint to Ireland, and that one of them— Tigris or Tigridia, had seventeen sons, all bishops, priests, and monks; and five daughters, all nuns: another—Darerca, had seventeen sons, all bishops, and two daughters : that another, called Lupita, was a virgin by one account, though a mother by another. Cinnenum or Ricella also had sons that became bishops, priests, and deacons; and that some of Darerca's sons belonged to Tigridia. He ought to have known that the groundwork or leading facts of a narration are often faithfully reported, though disfigured by popular tradition, or the fanaticism or credulity of the writers. Who would think of denying that St. Patrick had sailed to Ireland merely by reason of the ridiculous tradition, which says that Satan, moved to indignation by the foresight of the fruits of the Saint's mission, tried to sink the vessel on which he had embarked—first by dashing it against a sunken rock in the Clyde, opposite Kilpatrick, since called St. Patrick's rock,— and then by throwing at him, from the Kilpatrick hills, the rock on which now stands Dumbarton Castle; and, having missed him, as a last effort he threw after him Ailsa-Craig, which is to be seen in the mouth of the Frith of Clyde, between the coasts of Ayrshire and Kintyre. (71)

Things quite as marvellous as the origin and effects of the Trees' Well, and the miracles complained of, have been recorded of other saints without causing any one to doubt of their existence, at the places mentioned by the narrators of the miracles. The conception and nativity of St. John the Baptist were attended by miraculous events. There is at Rome, in the Mamertine prison, now converted into an oratory, a well miraculously produced during the incarceration there of SS. Peter and Paul, which supplied water for the baptism of their converts, the captains of their guards, SS. Processus and Mortinian, and forty-seven others. St. Emidius is recorded to have baptized Polisia, the daughter of the tyrant Polimius, who ordered his martyrdom, and one thousand others, inhabitants of Ausculum, with water which, like Moses, he had miraculously produced from a rock. By the Ostian Road, where St. Paul was beheaded, there are three fountains, of which the origin is said to have been miraculous, and a church is built over them. Yet no one has ever, on this account, denied that Zackary was in the temple in Jerusalem, or the Baptist born at Hebron; or that SS. Peter and Paul were in the Mamertine, or St. Emidius at Ausculum; or that St. Paul was beheaded not far from Rome, by the Ostian Road.

Even heretics admit the existence of miraculous or miracle-working powers in the Church, at its commencement, as necessary, or at least expedient, for the conversion of infidels, and cannot therefore, from principle alone, consistently deny the miraculous origin of the fountain in question.

Considering the matter in a Catholic point of view, Dr. Lanigan must admit that God has performed miracles both on account of, and by his saints, at times even when they were unconscious of their occurrence, and that he can do so again, as his power is not diminished nor restricted, and he has not revealed to us that he will never again exercise it in like manner. So that the credibility of a miraculous event, like other facts, depends upon the evidence of competent and truthful witnesses, and they are, therefore, to be admitted or rejected according as the evidence on which they rest is deemed sufficient or inadequate.

The faults of St. Patrick's boyhood are not necessarily an impediment to extraordinary manifestations of divine power in his infancy. Nor do such wonders misbecome the conversion of the Apostle of the Irish, more than those of the Jews, the Romans, or the people of Ausculum.

Any miracles ascribed to St. Patrick in his youth are not more incredible by reason of his having been born in Kilpatrick, than they would have been, had he been a native of Boulogne, or any other place. (72)

Whether this fountain was produced by a miracle, or sprung up by accident, from natural causes, at the time of St. Patrick's baptism, whether its water had a healing effect by the immediate interference of Providence, or had no such property, is of no consequence to my argument. The fact of its having been covered by a church, and mentioned as it is in the Office of the Church, is a clear proof of its having been regarded as a Holy Well, existing where St. Patrick was baptised. The well-known and immemorial practice of the Catholic Church of venerating, in a special manner, the places which bear the indications or are known to have been rendered remarkable by the immediate operation of the Divine beneficent power, coupled with these facts, is an additional corroboration of what I have endeavoured to demonstrate from history and tradition, viz., that St. Patrick was born at Kilpatrick. Now it may be useful to take a rapid retrospective view of the evidence hitherto adduced.

We learn from St. Patrick himself that he was a native of Great Britain, and born at Bonaven Taberniæ, which in Celtic means at the mouth of a river flowing into the Irish sea; from SS. Eleran and Evin, that he was of the Britons of Strathclyde; from St. Feich, that he was begotten in a tower, which the Aberdeen Breviary says was the Castle of Dumbarton. But as Dumbarton was not built when, according to the oldest authorities, St. Patrick was born, judging from the interpretation given to Emtur, we have seen it more probable that the tower referred to was the fort on Chapel-hill. St. Feich's commentator says that he was born in Dumbarton, but, like Dr. O'Connor, he has erred by an erroneous acceptation of the word " Ginear," which does not mean born but begotten; and his knowledge of the locality was evidently not very minute, for he makes no distinction between Alcluid or Dumbarton, and the fortress. SS. Patrick Junior, Benignus, Eleran, and Evin, tell us he was born in the walled town Nempthur. According to the Breviaries of Armagh and Paris this town was in Britain, and, as we have seen from the anonymous geographer of Ravenna, on the line of the wall of Antoninus. Jocelin maintains St. Patrick to have been born near Nemthor, and this agrees with the preceding statement—if Nempthor be taken in the sense that includes its suburbs, his description of St. Patrick's birth-place corresponds exactly with Kilpatrick. It was nearer the fortified station (Nemptor), on a lower eminence (Chapel-hill), than the castle on the promontory (Dumbarton), of which the ruins were visible in his day, and contiguous to the Irish Sea, in North Britain. This assertion is supported by the authority of the Aberdeen Breviary, which says that he was born at Kilpatrick; and by that of Probus, who assures us that the Saint's birth-place, Bannave Tyburnie, is the same as Arimuric or Dalmuir, the field of the wall, near the western sea, in the province of the towers, where the giants are said to have dwelt. There is here a slight difference between the statements of Probus and Jocelin. Probus says the birth-place of St. Patrick was (Haud procul a mari occidentali) not far from the western sea, and Jocelin has it (mari Hibernico collimitans) contiguous to the Irish Sea. The discrepancy is only apparent, and easily intelligible; for, when the tide is in, the Clyde at Kilpatrick becomes an estuary, and answers to Jocelin's description; when the tide is out it is only a river, and so corresponds to that given by Probus. This seeming difference then rather increases than diminishes the credibility of their assertions, and helps to mark more accurately the place which they described.

Thus we see that Bonaven Taberniæ, Empthoria, (and the other corruptions of Emporium,) Arimuric, and Kilpatrick, are but different successive names of the same place, expressive of its various conditions. Where the concurrent testimony of the oldest and the best authorities is so clear and explicit it is astonishing that any difference of opinion among modern writers does exist. Ignorance of the Celtic, and the diversity of the languages both of the writers and of the successive inhabitants of the place, together with the influence of a certain prejudice, can alone satisfactorily account for the discordant views entertained on a matter so very clearly attested.

The Trees' Well, in Kilpatrick, marks the place of the Saint's baptism; and as a church was subsequently built over it we are led to the conclusion that he was not baptised in a church, but in his father's house, where he was born. Thus we are enabled to say that St. Patrick was born (as near as can be seen by the Ordnance Survey map) in the 55°, 55′, 34″ N. Lat., and the 4°, 27′, 39″ W. Longitude.

Intimately connected with the question of St. Patrick's birth-place is that of the place whence he was led into captivity.

From the passage of the Confession first quoted, it appears that it was called Enon, and was a villa belonging to his father, situated not far from Bonaven Taberniæ, now Kilpatrick. Neither history nor tradition afford us any more definite information regarding the position of Enon, and therefore we must in our researches be guided by the faint light of etymology.

There is no place near Kilpatrick at present called Enon, nor do we know what lands in this district belonged to St. Patrick's father. Not far from Kilpatrick, *i.e.*, within about a mile of Dumbarton, on the high road to Cardross, there is a place which has preserved and perpetuated, for successive generations, the name given to St. Patrick in baptism— Succat. (73) That the domain once appertained to St. Patrick's father, Calpurnius, is suggested by the name. The estate of Succoth was, at a later period, the property of Sir Neil Campbell, married to Lady Mary, sister to King Robert Bruce. He died in 1316. (75) It was purchased, in 1616, by Robert Campbell. Sir Islay Campbell, President of the Court of Session, had the title of Succoth, and his son, Sir Archibald, having been made a judge, was designated Lord Succoth; (76) but as I cannot find any indication of its having, at any time, been called Enon, I cannot recognise it as the place mentioned in the Confession.

At the back of the Kilpatrick hills, to the north of Dumbarton Muir, lies Strath-Endrick, which derives its name from the river Endrick. In old Scotch songs it is called Innerdale, and by Frank, in his Northern Memoirs, (1694), Anderwick. In the Registry of the Priory of St. Andrew's it is called Innerwych. Now let us consider this word. Mr. Hughes, in his Geography of British History, sets down the terminations *rick* and *dale* as of Scandinavian origin, and *wich* as Roman: *rick* means a mountain ridge, and *dale* a valley; *wich*, the Latin *vicus*, a street. In the present case *rick* is applicable to the Campsie hills, and *dale* to the plain of the Endrick. Anderwick is but the Scoto-Saxon form of Innerwych, just as Hendrie stands for Henry, or Henricus. The Latin termination of Innerwych is a sufficient indication of its having been in the possession of the Romans, and consequently inhabited at a very early period. Now we have only to remove from the word Endrick, the terminations given it by the Romans, the Saxons, and the Danes, and restore its original Celtic termination On, a river; and we have Enon, the very word we are in search of. Here our attention is attracted by Baturick Castle, or Patrick's Castle, (77) situated on a rising ground about half-a-mile from Loch Lomond, and rather better than two miles from the hotel at Balloch. "It is presently the seat of Findlay of Easterhill, built on the ruins of an ancient castle of the same name, which seemed to have been once a magnificent edifice." (Gazetteer of Scotland, at Kilmaronock.) Its position on the east bank of Loch Lomond, beyond the wall of Antoninus, yet within the province of Valentia, out of sight of Kilpatrick and Dumbarton—let us understand how St. Patrick was here captured, while his parents escaped, being safe within the wall at Kilpatrick. The Irish pirates may have got access to that part of the country, as did the Danes in 1263, who sailed up Loch Long, and dragging their boats across the isthmus between Arrochar and Tarbert on Loch Lomond, rowed across the Lake and pillaged the adjoining district. This might easily have been done before succour could arrive from the Roman garrison at Kilpatrick or Dumbarton. As there is much truth in Mr. Chambers's remark that St. Patrick's progress may be traced by the names of the places called after him, I think that having identified Strath Endrick as Enon, we may fairly conclude that Baturick Castle is the very spot whence in his sixteenth year he was led into captivity by Nial Naoighiallach, or some other Irish pirate. It now only remains that I should account for the different other opinions which some modern writers have expressed as to the situation of St. Patrick's birth-place, and point out the causes which led them into error.

With Dr. Lanigan I account for the mistake of those who say that St. Patrick was born in Ireland, by observing that

they mistook the sense of the word Scotia in the martyrologies which have "In Scotia natiale S. Patricii," because
the term Scotia, or Scotland, had sometimes been applied to
Ireland. Yet it is certain that the saint was not born there,
because he tells us, in his Confession, that from his Irish
captivity he had to sail to his native country.

Others may have called him a Frenchman, because, as
Dempster relates, the Bretons of Armorica consider him their
fellow-citizen or countryman. They might well do so, in a
wide sense, in as much as they were also originally from
Great Britain. That St. Patrick was born at Boulogne is
not only erroneous as I have shown, but also quite a modern
theory unknown to the ancients: and the assertions that he
was born in Brittany or at Tours are refuted by Dr. Lanigan
and Mr. Hoey.

Dr. Lanigan and others have been led to believe that St.
Patrick was a native of France by their forced and false
construction of the expression used by Probus (in civitate
eorum Arimuric) "in their city Arimuric." They mistook
Arimuric for Armorica, notwithstanding that Probus had
called it a city. St Feich's scholiast seems also to have
partially fallen into this same error in the same way. For
though he gives Dumbarton, or Alcluith, as the birth-place
of the saint, yet he makes him be captured in Armorica,
contrary to the express words of the confession which say
he was taken from a villa near where he was born. It must,
however, in justice to the commentator be observed, that his
words, quoted by Dr. Lanigan as proof of his opinion, if we
abstract from the " trans mare Iccium" (which likely were
inserted in consequences of his mistake) are ambiguous—
Fecerunt prædas in Britanniæ Armoricæ, regione Letha, ubi
Patricius cum familia fuit." We have already met several
Celtic words having a Latin inflection and retaining their
Celtic signification. This passage may be translated either
" they ravaged the portion of the coasts of Britain called

Leith or Letha, where Patrick was with his family," or, "that they ravaged the district called Letha of Armoric Britain." Dr. Lanigan admits Letha to be the same as the British word Llydaw, which is applicable to any muddy shore. Camden calls Leith, Letha. Letavia or Letathia, not Letha, is the word commonly applied to the coast of Gaul I have met with no other reason assigned by any one to prove that St. Patrick was a native of France.

With reference to his having been born in Pembrokeshire, in Wales, the Bollandists remark that those who assert this are moved by envy of the Scotch, and seem to have no authority except Camden, who cautiously adds, however, "ut aliqui, nescio an vere scripserunt:"—"As some, with what truth I know not, have written." The Strathclyde Britons who settled in Wales of course claimed him, and truly, as their countryman; and, as he was born by the Clyde, succeeding generations may have naturally imagined that the Clyde in their new settlement was meant. There is another cause for this error, viz—that some mistook him for another St. Patrick, who, according to Butler, was older; and flourished and died among the hermits of Glastenbury, in Somersetshire; while others confound him with St. Petrock, founder of a monastery at Padstow, in Cornwall, who died at a much later period—on the 4th of June, about the year 564.

Thus there appear to be no solid grounds for asserting that St. Patrick was born in Ireland, in France, or in Wales; but as he must have been born somewhere, and as after a most diligent search I have found no evidence of his having been born anywhere else, I am compelled, for this reason, as well as for the others I have already enumerated, to believe that to Kilpatrick alone belongs by an unalienable right the honour of being the place of his nativity.

Probus relates a fact tending greatly to confirm the belief that St. Patrick was a Briton, which I must mention before concluding, for although it is not necessary for my proof, yet I should fail of doing justice to my subject were I to pass it by unnoticed.

On occasion of St. Patrick's demise the Britons to the east of Ireland threatened the people of Ulster with war for the purpose of removing the saint's body. Twice their fleet was prepared, and they were prevented, as Probus says, from shedding Christian blood, through the merits of St. Patrick and the mercy of God—on one occasion, by a storm that hindered the ships from encountering each other; on the other, by a fortunate delusion, or providential interference, while they were prepared for battle and rushing to the place of sepulture. (78) Such measures taken by the Britons can only be accounted for by their knowledge of his having been their countryman, and their conceiving that therefore they had a right to the possession of his sacred remains.

Their conduct, although more to be admired than imitated, evinced the sincerity of their attachment to St. Patrick, and their veneration for his relics. They marked their regard for his memory not only by the common adoption of his name, but also by the dedication of Churches to God in his honour.

Their devotion to him seems to have embraced also his friends and his instructors: for in the neighbourhood of East, or New Kilpatrick, Kilmardinny and German Loch still perpetuate the memory of St. Martin of Tours, and of St. Germanus of Auxerre, whose friendship he had cultivated, and whose doctrine he had imbibed during his sojourn in Gaul.

Whilst concluding this dissertation may I be permitted to express the hope, that the day is not far distant when the Irish, who received the Gospel light and the benefits of redemption through the ministry of St. Patrick, and the remnant of his Scottish countrymen, who with them have held for one thousand four hundred years, and still together hold uncorrupted, the faith professed and taught by St.

Patrick, and who have his memory in benediction, will emulate the devotion of their forefathers, and by their united efforts erect to the honour of St. Patrick, on the spot where he was baptized, a Church, that may be not only a perpetual mark of his birth-place, but, likewise, as of old, the resort of pilgrims; and the occasion of reviving piety, charity, and faith, in THIS HIS NATIVE LAND.

APPENDIX.

———•———

(1) See Dr. Lanigan's Ecclesiastical History of Ireland, vol. i., chap. iii., iv., vii. *passim*. My future references to this history, not otherwise expressed, will be to these chapters.

(2) " The theory most generally accepted, and which certainly has the greatest weight of authority in its favour, is that which assumes that St. Patrick was born in Scotland, at Dumbarton, on the Clyde." Essays on Religion and Literature, edited by Dr. Manning, pp. 108, 109.

(3) See the History of Ireland, p. 132, by Abbe MacGeoghegan.

(4) " The Iceni seem to have been Belgæ, from about the Iccius Portus, who, migrating wholly into Britain, left no trace behind them but the name. It was afterwards called also Bonona ; and it is remarkable that Benonæ was a town of the Iceni." Pinkerton's Enquiry into the early History of Scotland, chap. i., on Origins.

(5) " Gallorum Bononia eodem pene est etymo, quasi dicas Bon-avon sive Bon-aun." Baxter, Glossar. A., Britan ad Bonium.

(6) " Ego Patricius, peccator rusticissimus, et minimus omnium fidelium—patrem habui Calpurnium Diaconem (decurionem) filium quondam Potiti presbyteri qui fuit e vico Bonaven Taberniœ villam Enon prope habuit, ubi ego in capturam decidi." Conf. St. Patricii, Cap. I.

(7) " Gessoriacum Galli circa Constantini maximi principatum mutato nomine Bononiam vocare cœperunt." Hadrianus Vale-sius, Notitia Galliarum, at Gessoriacum.

(8) See Armstrong's Gælic Dictionary at Bun. To avoid the in-convenience of constant repetition, for such Celtic words as I may have occasion to use I refer my readers to this Dictionary ; and to the Gælic Dictionary, published by the Highland Society, and to O'Reilly's Irish Dictionary. It is almost impossible to trace the etymology, or to recognise the affinity of some Gælic words with cognate terms in other languages, without some knowledge of the peculiarities of Gælic orthography.

1. The letters a, o, u, are called broad vowels, and e, i, small vowels. 2. Plain consonants are aspirated by the placing of an h after them. The Irish use a dot (·) above the consonant, instead of an h after it. 3. In words of more than one syllable, the first vowel of each succeeding syllable must be of the same class with the last of its preceding syllable. Of this rule, Mr. Armstrong

says, in the preface to his dictionary :—" This mode of spelling is a modern invention. It was first introduced by the Irish, and adopted by the Gael, with, I confess, more precipitation than propriety. It has its advantages and disadvantages. It mars the primitive simplicity and purity of the language ; but it removes from it that appearance of harshness which arises from too great a proportion of consonants. It not unfrequently darkens somewhat the ground on which we trace the affinities of Gælic words with those of the sister dialects, and of other languages ; yet, it has infused into our speech a variety of liquid and mellow sounds, which were unknown, or at least not so perceptible before." 4. In the course of inflecting a primitive word, or combining a termination or compositive syllable therewith, if two vowels belonging to distinct syllables meet together, they must be separated by a silent dh, gh, or th. 5. The prefixes ó, es, im, in, di, are written éa, éu, eas, iom, ion, dio, before a broad root. 6. The letters c, d, g, l, n, r, s, t, and the aspirates ch, gh, dh, must be in juxtaposition to a broad or small vowel, according as they have their broad or narrow sounds.—See Munro's Gælic Grammar.

In order to obviate the difficulty arising from this orthography, I will (when the difficulty is manifest) give, as far as practicable, the phonetic spelling of the word, with the Latin or Italian sound of the vowels.

(9) See Keith Johnston's Classical Atlas.

(10) Gallia est omnis divisa in tres partes, quarum unam incolant Belgæ, aliam Aquitani, tertiam qui ipsorum lingura Celtæ, nostra Galli appellantur. Hi omnes lingua, institutis, legibus inter se differunt. Belgæ ab extremis Galliæ finibus oriuntur ; pertinent ad inferiorem partem fluminis Rheni."—De Bello Gallico, lib. i. sec. 1. Again Cæsar says, " Belgas ortos esse a Germanis. Lib. ii., chap. 4.

(11) Might not Boulogne be derived from Bun-uilt, *i.e.* the mouth of a brook? Bun-uilt, in the dialect which has Bon-avon, would likely be Bon-oilt. How could the letter l get into Boulogne from Bon-avon ?

(12) " In spelling compound words, if the syllabic accent be on the first syllable, the component parts must be incorporated into one undivided term—as òrcheard, a goldsmith." In spelling compounds of the above character, if the first term be feminine, the initial consonant of the second term must be aspirated ; but, if the first term be of the masculine gender, the initial consonant of the second remains plain, as fearciùil, a musician."—Munro's Gælic Grammar, pp. 6, 7.

(13) The word *Provincia* had now become low Latin for a region, land, or territory, however large. Per Gallicanum Provinciam— Galliarum provinciis. Provincia mundus ipse dicitur. Tertull. adv. Valent. c. 20.—See Pinkerton's Enquiry, vol. i., p. 316.

(14) " Sanctus Patricius, qui et Socket vocabatur, Brito fuit natione. Hic in Britaniis natus est—de vico Bannavæ Tyburniæ regionis, haud procul a mari occidentali, quem vicum indubi-

tanter comperimus e·se Nevtri.e (Nentriæ) provinciæ, in qua olim gigantes habitasse dicuntur." Lib. i. cap. 1.

Mr. Hocy quotes the passage thus—" Brito fuit natione—de vico Bannave Tiburniæ regionis, hand procul a mari occidentali—quem vicum indubitanter comperimus esse Neustriæ provinciæ, in qua olim gigantes," omitting the clause which tells us of St. Patrick's nativity in Britain, and giving us not Probus's word, but Linigan's interpretation, Neustria.

(15) An. the,

	Singular.		Plural.
	Mas.	Fem.	Mas. and Fem.
Nom.	An, Am	An, a',	Na,
Gen.	An, a',	na,	Nam, Nan,
Dat.	An, 'n, a',	an, a'	Na.

Strictly speaking the viriations of the article are only an, na, nan—am, a' 'n, nam, are forms which it assumes *causa euphoniæ*," and are determined by the letter that precedes or follows them. Munro's Gælic Grammar, p. 49.

The definite article is now written in Irish and Scotch Gælic with the vowel a. It was formerly written with e, v, gr., " Al-necluid," the rock of the Clyde—Fordun, xi., 29. But it still retains the indistinct sound of e, heard in the French particle *ne*. In the book of Ballymote I find also i instead of e, or a, used in the article. " In tseiscad brathar."

To restore the article to its ancient form we have only to replace a by e, and then we have en, em, ne, nen, nem.

(16) See lectures on the Science of Language, p. 303, by Max Müller.

(17) The euphonic particle *an* or *am* is inserted between the preposition ann (in), and a noun singular or plural, used indefinitely, —as *Ann an tigh*, in a house; *Ann am baile.* (3) Before the article or relative ann is written *anns*, as anns an tigh (in the house). (3) Very often the preposition is elided, as *am' bail eile*, in another town. The elipsis is always left unmarked ; but as *an* and *am* may in this connection be mistaken for the article, they should be written '*am*, '*an*, for the sake of distinction ; as *am bail' eile*, the other town ; '*am bail' eile*, in the other town." Munro's Gælic Grammar, p. 194.

(18) See D'Anville's map of the countries of Western Europe during the middle ages, published by George Philips and Son, 32, Fleet-street, London, which shows Boulogne in Flandria, in Austrasia ; and Neustria, lying between Austrasia and the Loire.

" D'Anville, Jean Baptist Bourguignon, first geographer to the King of France, member of the Academy of Inscriptions and Belles Lettres, of the Antiquarian Society of London, and adjoint geographer to the Parisian Academy of Sciences, born at Paris, 1697. D'Anville devoted his whole life to geographical studies, and the numerous valuable maps and works he published, left him without a rival. He published 78 treatises and 211 maps, all of which arc distinguished for their accuracy and perspicuity." Maunder's Biographical Treasury.

(19) " Cæteræqne civitates positæ in ultimis Galliæ finibus, occeano conjunctæ ; quæ Armoricæ appellantur."—Hirtius, de Bello Gallico, lib. viii, sec. 25.

(20) " Gallos ab Aquitanis Garumna flumen, a Belgis Matrona et Sequana dividit."—Cæsar, de Bello Gallico, lib i., sec. 1.

(21) " Per tractum Belgicæ et Armoricæ."—Eutropius, lib. xix.

(22) See D'Anville's Map of Ancient Gaul.

" Armorica, which word in the Celtic language signified a mari·time country, comprised that part of Celtic Gaul which is now divided into Brittany, Lower Normandy, Anjou, Main, and Touraine." Lives of the Saints, vol. i., p. 382, by Rev. A. Butler.

(23) Hi inter Gessoriacenses Ambianosque medii, in ora similiter positi ea loca tenuere certe, ubi nunc oppida Stapulæ, Monstrolium, Hesdinium et adjacentem agrum Ponticum, *Le Ponthieu* ad Sommanam amnen."—Hardion.

See, also, D'Anville's Map of Ancient Gaul.

(24) " In 1304, the law of the Scots and Brets is mentioned in an instrument quoted by Sir David Dalrymple, in his Annals. These Brets were probably the Britons of Strath-Clyde, as all the northern writers call the Welsh Brets, and Wales Bretland. 1. Winton, also, uses Bret and Bretan, for Briton and Britain. Nay, in Clydesdale at present, if you will ask the common people about any ancient castle, or the like, they will tell you it was erected by the Brets, or by the Pects, that is by the Britons, or by the Picks. The Notitia Imperii uses Britti for Britons ; the Saxon translation of Beda, Brytta. Witicind, in the Gesta Saxonum, uses Bracti often for Britons. 2. Snorro and the Icelandic Sagas call Wales Bretland, and its people Brets. The Saxon Chronicle calls the Welsh Bryttar. Fordun, ix., 56, mentions " Albaniæ Britones."—Pinkerton, vol. i., p. 81.

By the Scotch Celts their country is still called *Albainn*, from *Al*, a rock, and *Beinn*, a mountain. They know Scotland by no other name. Britain they call *Breatann* (pron. Bretun).

(25) History of Ireland, p. 92. By Abbe MacGeoghegan.

(26) Lanigan, vol. i., pp. 135, 137.

(27) He might as well have said the Archipelago, as the words used in the Annals of Ireland " muir n ioct," apparently mean a sea abounding with islands, most probably the inner Hebrides were meant. What gives occasion to such mistakes is, that those who make them are often better skilled in classical languages than in their own. Ioct from i, an island, and och, or ach, a termination indicating plurality, as eilean, an island ; eileanach, an archipelago.

(28) "Hiberione (*i.e.* Hibernia) in captivitate abductus sum, cum tot millibus hominum secundum merita nostra quia a deo recessimus, et sacerdotibus nostris non obedientes fuimus, qui nostram salutem admonebant, &c." Conf. S. Patricii, ed. Ware, p. 1.

(29) " Ut pergens in Britannias, et libentissime paratus eram, quasi ad patriam et parentes ; non id solum ; sed eram (paratus)

usque Gallias visitare fratres, et ut viderem faciem sanctorum Domini mei."—Conf. p. 17. Ware, 1 Ed.

(30) See W. Hughes's Geography of British History, p. 72.

(31) Tacitus says—" Summotis velut in aliam insulam hostibus." Writing of the Picts and Scots of Argyle, Bede has : " Transmarinas autem dicimus has gentes, non quod extra Britanniam essent positæ, sud quia a parte Britonum erant remotæ duobus finibus maris interjacentibus.—Lib. i, c. 12.

(32) " Unde autem (possem) etsi voluero dimittere illas et pergere in Britannias; etsi libentissime paratus, irem quasi ad patriam et parentes ; et non id solum, sed etiam usque ad Gallias visitarem fratres meos ut viderem faciem sanctorum Domini mei.—Confessio B. Patricii, apud Acta SS. Bolland. tom. ii. Martii, p. 537.

' "Iterum post paucos annos in Britannia eram cum parentibus meis, qui me ut filium exceperunt, et ex fide rogaverunt me, ut vel modo post tantas tribulationes quas ego pertuli nunquam ab illis discederem."—Ibid, p. 535. In Britanniis eram, aliud exemplar apud O'Connor, Rer. Hib. Script. tom. i., p. 111 ; Proleg. i.

(33) " Et manu mea scripsi atque condidi verba ista danda ac tradenda militibus mittenda Corotici, non dico civibus meis, atque civibus sanctorum Romanorum, sed civibus dæmoniorum ob mala opera ipsorum, &c.

Ingenuus fui secundum carnem, decurione patre nascor. Vendidi enim nobilitatem meam. Non erubesco, neque me pœnitet pro utilitate aliorum. Denique servus sum in Christo Jesu Domino nostro, etsi mei me non cognoscunt. Phropheta in patria sua honorem non habet." S. Patricii Epistola ad Coroticum apud O'Connor, Rer. Hib. Script. tom. i., p. 117. Proleg. i.

(34) " Natus est Patricius Nemturri," for so Dr. O'Connor translates the old and original Irish—Genair Patraic i Nemthur. Cormen vetus Hibernicum Feici apud O'Connor.—Rer. Hib. Script. tom. i., p. 90. Pro leg. i. Neamh-thur Hibernica vox est quæ cœlestem, sive altam turrim denotat, aliter Hibernice dictam Alcluid rupes Cluidensis, hodie Dumbarton. Vetus scholiastes hujus carminis qui Neamh-thur et Alcluid unam et camdem civitatem esse declarat, uti Jocelinus et Evinus.—Ibid, p. 98.

(35) Profectus est (Patricius) trans Alpes omnes.
Trans maria, fuit felix expeditio
Et remansit apud Germanum
In Australi parte Australis Lethaniæ.
Carmen Feici, strop. 5. Ibid, p. xci. Lethaniam appellabant Hiberni non modo Armoricam, sed et occidentalem Galliam.—Ibid, in notis.

(36) In historical importance, I consider this life next to the writings of St. Patrick, because the writer follows, as Dr. Lanigan admits, the authority of SS. Columbkill, Ultan, Adamnan, Eleran the Wise, Kearan of Belachduin ; of Hermedus, bishop of Clogher, Colman Huamacensis, and Colatus—a priest of Driumrelgeach, in Meath. This Life, partly in Latin, but mainly in Irish, was translated by Colgan and his assistants.—I cite the Lives in Colgan's

collection by the names of the authors to whom they are ascribed, merely for the sake of distinction.

(37) " Civitas Britonum munitissima usque hodie, quæ vocatur Alcluith, L. i.   Alcluith quod lingua eorum significat Petram Cluith ; est enim juxta fluvium nominis illius. Beda, i. 12, et vide 26, (A.D. 731.)

(38) The old Roman Breviary has—" Genere Brito ;" present— " Majori in Britannia natus ;" Br. of the canons of Lateran—" Ex Britannia magna insula;" Rheims—" In maritimo Britanniæ terri- torio;" Paris—"In Britannia natus, oppido Empthoria ;" Armagh— " In illo Britanniæ oppido nomine Emptor;" SS. Patrick Junior and Benignus—" Natus est igitur in illo oppido, Nempthur nomine. Patricius natus est in campo Taburniæ" ; St. Eleran—" In oppido Nempthur, quod oppidum in campo Taberniæ est." See Mr. Hoey's Essay.

(39) " The Life of St. Patrick," written in Latin, by Jocelin, a Cambro-Briton, and monk of Furness, is, according to Usher, the most ample and correct that has been published.   This author had followed the other Lives of St. Patrick, which had been written before his time ; and had at least seen some of them, as he quotes the four books of the four disciples of the saint—namely, of St. Benignus, St. Mel, St. Luman, and St. Patrick, with that of St. Evin.   He composed his history, as he himself asserts, at the soli- citation of Thomas or Tomultach O'Connor, archbishop of Ard- mach ; Malachi, bishop of Down ; and John Curcy, Prince of Ulidia,—after those original Lives, from which he extracted every- thing worthy of being related."—History of Ireland, p. 134, by Abbe MacGeoghegan.

(40) " Extitit vir quidam Calphurnius nomine, filius Potiti pres- byteri, Brito natione, in pago Taburnia vocabulo (hoc est, taberna- culorum campo ; eo quod Romanus exercitus tabernacula fixerat ibidem) secus oppidum Nempthor degens, mari Hibernico collimi- tans habitatione.   Hic duxerat in matrimonium puellam Francige- nam Conquessam nomine. . . . . forma atque morum elegantia egregiam.   De Galliis namque abductam cum sorore priore natu, ad Aquilones partes Britanniæ et in obsequium patris sui venditam adamavit, ejusque delectus moribus, . . . illam ex ancillari famulatu in conjugale consortium promovit.   Soror vero illius alteri tradita viro, habitabat in Nempthor oppido prænominato." Caput. I.   Cœlitus edoctus et eductus, de terra et cognatione sua, et de domo patris sui cum fideli Abraham exivit, natale solum Britanniæ pertransiens, Galliarum fines adivit."   Cap. iii.   Erat autem in quodam promontorio supereminenti præfato oppido Nem- thor munitio quædam extructa, cujus adhuc apparent minora ves- tigia. V. viii. Vita S. Patricii auctore Jocelino, monacho de Furnesio. Acta sanctorum, Martii, tom. ii., f. 517, 540, 554.

(41) " This Breviary is the only existing one proper to Scotland, and is therefore of importance to those who regard with interest such an authentic record of the ancient forms and usages of the Scottish Church.   It has also some claims on account of its histo-

rical and literary value. That great care was bestowed by Bishop
Elphinstone and his assistants in preparing the work for the press
is evident. In regard to the legends of the saints, it forms the
chief source from which the Bollandists and Scottish martyrologists
have derived their information ; and its general accuracy has been
tested by comparison of passages which are quoted from Beda and
other early writers, whose works still exist. On this head, in the
prospectus of this recapitulation, it is remarked :—" The fragments
of biography, indeed the legends and hymns which are here en-
shrined, preserve under the seal of Church authority much more
than is elsewhere recorded of the greatest event in the history of
Scotland—the conversion of her tribes to the Christian faith. In
the instances of some of the chief missions, such as those of St.
Ninian and St. Columba, St. Kentigern, and St. Serf, the original
materials employed in the preparation of the work have, in whole
or in part, descended to our own day, and the remarkable fidelity
with which we find these cited in its pages, warrant us in placing
a high value upon the accounts that are given of other apostles and
early teachers, of whose pious enterprise every other memorial has
passed away. The frequent details of this kind which the Breviary
supplies, are scarcely more interesting, in their unlooked-for novelty,
than in their characteristic minuteness, which is such as not unfrequently to surprise the provincial, or even the parochial antiquarian,
by the commemoration of places once venerable in the religious
associations of the people, but now so forgotten that the significant
names, which were then impressed upon them, have long ceased to
be understood."—Preface, by David Laing, to Toovey's edit. of the
Aberdeen Breviary, London, 1854. The Aberdeen Breviary was
prepared and completed for publication under the special superin-
tendance of William Elphinstone, bishop of Aberdeen, who founded
there King's College in 1494, and died in 1514, aged 83. The
Breviary was first printed by W. Chepman, 1509–1510, in Edin-
burgh.

(42) " Patricius Hybernensium apostolus ex patre Calphurnio de
Scotorum nobili familia ortus, Conchessa matre, beati Martini
Turonensi Episcopi Francigena sorore, apud castellum Dunbertanæ,
in alvo matris præsagiis conceptus et in Kilpatrick prope idem castellum in Scotia natus et educatus extitit in baptismate Suthat a
comparentibus nominatus : post hoc a sancto Germano in Gallia
Magonius, et a beato Celestino papa Romæ, Patricius appelatus."

(43) " The Life of St. Patrick, by Probus, in two books, is a very
valuable work. Colgan, indeed, was not friendly to it, because, he
says, it does not agree, especially in the first book, with some of the
other lives. This is the very reason why it is far preferable to
them. It has nothing about Colgan's favourite visionary town
Nempthor in North Britain, but quite the reverse ; nor any of the
foolish miracles attributed to St. Patrick when a child, in the
tracts, to which Colgan was most uncritically partial. The author
sticks very closely to the Confession and the letter against Coroticus. The Bollandists, otherwise sharp enough with regard to the

Lives of St. Patrick, yet looked upon this by Probus as very useful, particularly towards a regular arrangement of the acts of our Saint." Lanigan, Vol. i. c. 111.

(44) " Reverterunt ergo impudentes grassatores Hiberni domum post non multum tempus reversuri. Picti vero in extrema parte insulæ tunc primum et deinceps quieverunt ; prædas tamen non nunquam exinde de Britonum gente agere non cessarunt." Beda, i, 14. See, also, Tacitus, Dio, Nennius, Camden, Pinkerton, Hughes's Geography of British History, Horseley's Britannia Romana, Roy's Military Antiquities, George Chalmers' Caledonia, and the Gazetteer of Scotland.

(45) " Ex-gr. Patricius filius Calphurnii, filii Potiti, filii Odissii, filii Gorniæ, filii Menchidii, filii Leonis, filii Maximi, filii Hencreti, filii Ferini, filii Briti, a quo Britanni Nominati sunt."

(46) " Cæsar, also, mentions this practice of the Britons, "Omnes vero se Britanni vitro inficiunt, quod cœruleum efficit colorem ; atque hoc horibiliores sunt in pugno aspectu." De Bello Gallico, lib. v., cap. 14.

(47) " Cum meliorem Britanniæ partem imperio suo Romani subegissent, eam vero quam subjugare non potuerunt primum Adrianus imperator ducto ad tutelam vallo adjunxisset, hoc non sufficiente, Severus aliud minus remotum struxit, trans illud reliquit eos Britones, quos ex re Pictos Latine nominatos credibile est, juxta veteris nominis Brith significationem, proptera quod corpora cœruleo colore tingebant. Extendebatur autem diœcesis sua (adcoque et Ternani diœcesis) secundum limites Cambrensi regni ; a muro scilicet illo famoso ad arcendum hostes (Pictos et Scotos) a Britonibus, a mari (Hibernico) ad mare (Germanicum) olim constructo usque ad flumen Fordense, &c."—A. SS. Junii, t. ii., (De Sancto Ternano, Pictorum in Britannia Episcopo.)

(48) Unless Bracti, which occurs in Whiticind's Gesta Saxonum be derived from the German Brachen, which, in that case, would be applicable only to that portion of the Britons who lived in marshy fields or fens.

(49) " The boundary of the country which the bravery of the emigrants won, would be tolerably well defined by a line drawn from Chester through Holt, Wexham, Oswestry ; and turning to Mold by Ruthin, and Denbigh, to the sea. The descendants of the emigrants who dwell in Flintshire, and in the vale of Cluyd, are distinguished from their neighbours by a remarkable difference of person and speech. They are a people taller, slenderer, and with longer visages ; their voices are smaller and more shrill. They have many varieties of dialect, and generally their pronunciation is less open than what is heard from the Welsh, who live to the westward of them." See Welsh Chron. of the Princes Caradoc.— Welsh Archælog., vol. ii., p. 482.

(50.) " Thus, in a MS. of the Cotton Library, Nero E. I. we find Didanus Rex Oxenfordiæ, for king of Mercia. In Caradoc of Lancarvon, under the year 933, we find King of London put for

King of England; and the same expression is used in the laws of Howel Dha." Pinkerton's Enquiry, vol. i., p. 71.

(51) "Nemthur est civitas in Britannia septenbrionali nempe Alcluida."

(52) In the original Celtic the name is Fion, and I do not know why M'Pherson has translated it Fingal, unless he confounded Fion Mac Chomhail, King of Morven, with Fiongal, King of the Dalriads, or Dalreudini, of Kintyre.

Morven is literally the great mountains, or what is now called in Gaelic "Na Garbh-Chriochan," *i.e.*, the Rough Bounds, which includes the whole of the west of Scotland, from Loch Torridan, about the middle of Rosshire.

Fion appears to have been Finnanus, the tenth on the list of our Scottish kings. If I might follow the example of Keating, in his compilation of the History of Ireland, and be permitted to correct our Chroniclers by tradition and the authority of the Bards, at a period of which we have no authentic record, I should say that Finnanus was not the son, but the father of Josina, or Ossian, so that the list would be, Conanus, Finnanus, Josina Drustus, &c. Finnanus was buried at Beregonium, supposed to be the Selma of Ossian, about four miles north of Dunstaffnage, in the parish of Ardchattan, Argyleshire. The grave of Fiongal, King of the Dalriads, whom tradition assures us to have been a cruel tyrant, very different from Fion, is, to this day, pointed out by the natives at Saddel, nine miles to the north of Campbelltown, in Kentire.

' Richard of Cirencester says, A.M. 3650, by his calculation A.C. 350, "Circa hæc tempora in Hiberniam commigrarunt ejecti a Belgis Brittones ibique sedes posuerunt, ex illo tempore Scotti appellati." *Vide* Pinkerton, vol. xi., p. 35.

The Scotts were separated from the Picts by the chain of mountains called Dorsum Britannicum, or the highest part of ancient Braidalban. Pinkerton, vol. i., p. 315.

(53) See the Ordnance Survey of Scotland, sheets No. 30 and 31. "Fergus, the first king of the Scots, divided his possessions by lot among his chiefs after the battle of Dune. By this means each of them being placed as his chance fell they inhabited their quarters with such people as they had the leading of, so that afterwards the countries took their names of those the first governors, which names for the more part (being a little changed) remain among them even unto this day."—Scottish Chronicle, by Raphael Hollinshed, vol. i., p. 43.

(54) In the eighteenth century M'Pherson's translation of Ossian's Poems was by many of the learned scouted as a forgery, mainly by reason of the supposed impossibility of transmitting such long poems by oral tradition through so many generations. In the nineteenth century the literati of Europe received without a murmur, or suspicion, from the Finns, a similar composition, transmitted to posterity in exactly the same way.

" The Finns are the most affected member of the whole family, and are, the Magyars excepted, the only Finnic race that can claim a station among the civilised and civilising nations of the world. Their literature, and, above all, their popular poetry, bear witness to a high intellectual development in times which we may call mythical, and in places more favorable to the glow of poetical feelings than their present abode—the last refuge Europe could afford them. The epic songs still live among the poorest, recorded by oral tradition alone, and preserving all the features of a perfect metre, and of more ancient language. A national feeling has lately arisen among the Finns, despite the Russian supremacy, and the labours of Sjögern, Lömrot, Castren, and Killgren, receiving hence a powerful impulse, have produced results truly surprising. From the mouths of the aged an epic poem has been collected equalling the Iliad in length and completeness—nay, if we can forget for a moment all that we in our youth learned to call beautiful, not less beautiful. A Finn is not a Greek, and Wainamoinen was not a Homer. But if the poet may take his colours from that nature by which he is surrounded, if he may depict the men with whom he lives, Kalemala possesses merits not dissimilar from those of the Iliad, and will claim its place as the fifth national epic of the world, side by side with the Ionian songs, with the Mahábhárata, the Shahnámah, and the Nihelunge."—Science of Language, by Max Müller, vol. i., p. 330.

(55) Attacotti, i.e., Athaic-chogaidh, which means giants of war. The Romans had to learn their name not by its letters but by its sound. Ammianus says, "Attacotti bellicosa hominum natio." In his Archæologia Britannica, Lluyd has "Athaic-thuatha," gigantes septentrionales.—Vide O'Connor, Proleg. xi., 71.

(56) "Cum adhuc esset in patria sua cum patre Calpurnio et matre Conchessa fratre etiam Ructi et sorore Mila nomine, in civitate corum Arimuric facta est seditio magna in partibus illis. Nam filii Rethmiti regis de Britannia vastantes Arimuric.— Probus, liv. i., c. 12.

(57) We do not read of the Caledonians having joined with the Irish in an invasion on any part of the coasts of France.

(58) It is not improbable that national vanity, and the contest for priority of rule, between the kings of England and Scotland, may have induced our historians to represent as successive sovereigns in their catalogues of Pictish and Scottish kings, rulers who contemporaneously governed different parts of the country; while tradition and poetry, their principal guides, for the most part void of accurate chronology and geography, justly styled by Pinkerton, "the eyes of history," greatly favored such a prevarication. The early history of all ancient nations is inaccurate, and often fabulous.

(59) Balclutha is commonly asserted to be the fort of Dunbarton. But the statement seems incorrect; for Jocelin says that Finan M'Con lived upwards of a hundred years before St. Patrick; and in this he is supported by Gibbon, and the Irish historians. Balclutha was destroyed by Fion's father, Comhal, and, consequently, long before Dumbarton was built. Kilpatrick was then the only

town on the Clyde, possessed by the Romanised Britons, accessible to ships, and, therefore, it is not improbable that Reuthámir's house, the scene of the combat between Clessámnor and Renda, was the fort of Dunglass.

(60) The word *Airidh* (pr. Ari) a shealing, or summer residence, is derived from a Gælic word now obsolete, *Ar*, *i.e.* earth. Akin to it are the words *ar*, to plough, and *Araich*, a field—in O'Reilly's Irish Dictionary it is written Ara.—Lat. Arvum,—Gr. Aρυρα. It is a component part of the names of several places in Scotland, as Arihaunda, Arihualain: *i.e.* Airidhshaundra, Airidhshualain.

(61) See the History of Dumbartonshire, by Joseph Irving, p. 75, where mention is made of a grant, by Robert III., "to St. Patrick's chapel, in the Castle at Dumbarton, of ten marks sterling, yearly, out of the town mails of Dumbarton; and a precept directed to the bailies of said burrow commanding them to pay the ten marks yearly."

(62) It is not easy to fix the exact date of St. Patrick's birth, as it can only be determined by the date of his death, and the length of his life, of which we have nine different statements by various authorities. He was born, A.D. 344, according to the oldest British writer, Nennius, who says that he lived one hundred and twenty years, and died fifty-seven years before the birth of St. Columba, which took place, A.D. 521. All the oldest authorities concur in assigning 120 years of life to St. Patrick. He was said to have been in four respects like Moses. 1. An angel spoke to both from a bush. 2. Both fasted forty days. 3. Both lived one hundred and twenty years. 4. The places of their interment were unknown. (St. Patrick's body was found in 1185 in a church bearing his name at Down, in Ulster). Dr. Lanigan admits the attestation of those parities between Moses and St. Patrick to have been older than the lives we have of the Saint, and even more ancient than St. Feich's hymn, vol. i., p. 356. Latter writers, Baronius, Petavius, and others, have supposed that by mistaking L for C; some copyist in transcribing St. Patrick's life, by Probus, had changed LXXXII into CXXXII. This, however, is but a gratuitous assumption. Others take occasion to deny him the last thirty years of life assigned, because during that time they do not find any important acts which he performed. But it is unreasonable to expect public acts from a man over ninety years of age. A more rational objection might be made to the statements of the ancients from the ordinary duration of human life; but even that rule admits of exceptions, and certainly the weight of authority in favour of the one hundred and twenty years is very great.

(63) Iterum sunt civitates in ipsa Britannia ubi plus augustissima de oceano in oceano esse dignascitur. Id est Velunia, Volitanio, Pexa, Begese, Calanica, Medio, Nemeton, Subdobiadon, Litana, Cibra, Credigone. Another version is—" In ipsa Britannia in recto tramite una alterius connexæ ubi et ipsa Britannia plus augustissima, 307, l. 1. Medionemeton, &c.—Geographi Gr. min. tom. iii. Variæ Lectiones, Anon. Ravennatis, ex codice Vaticano

cum ed 1688, Paris, 306, lib. 3.—See Pinkerton's Enquiry, vol. i., app., p. 430.

(64) In illo Britanniæ oppido nomine Emptor."—Brev. Arm. " In Britannia natus oppido Empthoria."—Brev. Parisien.

(65) Not only in Irish but also in Latin manuscripts was the preposition often joined to the noun. The Scotch Episcopalian Bishop of Brichen, Dr. Forbes, in his preface to his edition of the Arbuthnot Missal, gives thus the following prayer from a manuscript (in an Irish handwriting) of the book of Deer, preserved in the Cambridge University Library—" Creator naturarum omnium deus et parens universarum incelo etinterra originum has trementis populi tui relegiosas preces exillo inacessibileis lucis trono tuo suscipe etinterhiruphin etzaraphin indefcssas circumstantium laudes exaudi spei nonambigue precationes.—p. 15.

(66) " What is more worthy of attention is the fact that the Church of the parish (of Kilpatrick) was a place of pilgrimage previous to the twelfth century, for we have evidence that before that epoch, Alwin, Earl of Lennox, had confirmed to the Church of Kilpatrick all the lands of Cochinach, Edinbernan, Baccan, &c, which had been granted *by his predecessors*, and had himself added the land of Cateconnen. There is evidence that at the end of the twelfth century these lands were held by a person called Beda Ferdan, (who lived at Monachkenneran on the Clyde, in a house of wattle,) and three other persons who were bound for all service *to receive and entertain strangers coming to the Church of St. Patrick*." The Labourer, 1865, Sept., p. 270.

(67) See Hughes's Geography of British History, and Chalmers's Caledonia.

(68) Statistical Account of Scotland, vol. iv., p. 229, by John Sinclair, Bart., 1793.

(69) Qui (Patricius) baptismatis unda noviter regeneratus divino admonitus instinctu dum manu sua dextera crucis signaculum humo imprimeret amœnissimus fons inde scaturizavit. Unde quidam gormias nomine a nativitate cœcus oculos et faciem ex ejusdem fontis latice lavans non tantum videndi exterius actum recepit sed et litteras legendi et intelligendi licet illiteratus aparte cognovit et sic de exteriore beneficio factus est de cœco videns et interiore gratia de illiterato litteratus lapisque in super fontem illum juxta existens quociens falcidicus testis aut perjurus super illum manum posuerit effundere aquam consuevit."—17 Mart. St. Patricius, Lec. 11, Brev. Aberd.

(70) " On the 28th of November, 1630, Margaret Davidson, a married woman, residing in Aberdeen, was adjudged in an unlaw of five pounds by the Kirk Session, ' for directing her nurse with her bairn to St. Fiack's Well, and washing her bairn therein for recovery of her health, and for leaving an offering in the well.' The prevalence of this custom is indicated by the decree of the Session on the same day, threatening heavy censures and punishment to all who should be found going to Saint Fiack's Well, for seeking health to themselves or bairns."—Chambers's Domestic

Annals of Scotland, vol. i., p. 323, where several other similar instances are recorded.

(71) Ailsa Craig is a mass of columnar syenetic trap, shooting up in a conical form to an altitude of 1,100 feet, according to Macculloch, from an elliptical base of 3,300 feet in the major axis, by 2,200 in the minor—Imperial Gazeteer of Scotland, p. 27.

The Historian of Dumbartonshire beautifully illustrates the Protestant idea of the *cultus sanctorum*, or veneration of saints, when he expresses his fear of being thought irreverent for relating in a note the action of the powers of darkness on the Rock of Dumbarton, after having in the text scoffingly told how in his second captivity, St. Patrick had been sold for a common kettle. I should like to know why Protestants think it more irreverent to mention Satan, than to ridicule the Saints of God.

(72) We do not now hear of miracles being wrought at the Trees' Well. It is not easy to determine whether this arises from want of virtue in the water, or want of faith in the recipients. Without claiming for it any supernatural virtue, it is a remarkable fact at the present day, that its water is by the inhabitants of Kilpatrick considered the best in the place, although it is situated only a few paces from the grave-yard, and on the declivity of the ground.

(73) In the Aberdeen Breviary this name is written Suthat; by Probus, Socket; by Stanihurst, Sochar; in the second life, Succet; in the Tripartite, Suchat; by St. Feich, Succat; by Usher, Succath.

(74) See the Scottish Nation, by Wm. Anderson.

(75) See Transactions of the Society of Scottish Antiquities. vol. ii., part i., p. 213.

(76) In order to perceive the identity of Patrick and Baturick it is only necessary to observe that the British used B for P, as appears by the names already mentioned of the places in Wales called after St. Patrick, and that the u in Baturick is retained from the Scoto-Irish Padruig.

(77) " In tempore transitus sanctissimi patris nostri Patricii, dira quædum belli contentio inter Orientales Britanniæ populos ex una parte, et inter ultanos ex altera parte orta est de tullendo corpore ejusdem sanctissimi veri in loco qui collum bovis nominatur ; sed meritis beati Patricii, et misericordia Dei, ne sanguis effundaretur Christianorum seditio illico sedata est. Condicto enim bellorum die, intumescebant ultra fluctus maris, quod erat inter insulanos istos, prohibentes naves bellicas ne ad invicem convenire ullatenus potuissent. Alio autem tempore cum quievissent maria, surrexerunt iterum orientales contra ultanos populos, et acriter ad certamen irruerunt, et certatim armati in bellum hostiti impetu ad locum beati corporis proruerunt, sed felici mirabiliter sunt fallacia seducti." Probus, in vita S. Patricii, inter opera Bedæ, vol. iii. p., 334.

THE END.

www.ingramcontent.com/pod-product-compliance
Lightning Source LLC
Chambersburg PA
CBHW031246260626
47169CB00007B/2469